Dirty Bertie

A DOLLOP of DISASTER

DAVID ROBERTS WRITTEN BY ALAN MACDONALD

Collect all the
Dirty Bertie books!

Contents

STRIPES PUBLISHING
An imprint of the Little Tiger Group
1 The Coda Centre, 189 Munster Road,
London SW6 6AW

A paperback original
First published in Great Britain in 2014

ISBN: 978-1-84715-448-4

Characters created by David Roberts
Text copyright © Alan MacDonald
Fetch! 2010 • Kiss! 2009 • Ouch! 2011
Illustrations copyright © David Roberts
Fetch! 2010 • Kiss! 2009 • Ouch! 2011

The right of Alan MacDonald and David Roberts to
be identified as the author and illustrator of this work
respectively has been asserted by them in accordance
with the Copyright, Designs and Patents Act, 1988.

Printed and bound in the UK.

10 9 8 7 6 5 4 3 2

Dirty Bertie

FETCH!

For Julia, Edward and Mickey-Love

~ D R

For Zoe, Ed, Arthur, Maisie and Tess the dog

~ A M

Contents

CHAPTER 1

DING DONG.

"Bertie, can you get that?" called Mum.
Bertie scooted into the hall and
opened the front door.

"Special delivery!" said the postman,
handing him a brown parcel.

It was addressed to Master Bertie
Burns. Wait a minute — that was him!

"I GOT A PRESENT! I GOT A PRESENT!" he yelled, bursting into the kitchen.

"It's not fair!" grumbled Suzy. "Why didn't *I* get anything?"

"Cos no one likes you," said Bertie, sticking out his tongue.

Mum was looking at the postmark. "It must be a late birthday present. I think it's from Uncle Ed in America."

Bertie gasped. Rich Uncle Ed? He sent the coolest presents – even if they never arrived on time. Bertie tore off the wrapping paper. He stared. It *wasn't*! It *couldn't* be!

Dirty Bertie

"Ha ha! It's a toy dog," said Suzy.

"No it isn't, it's a ROBODOG!" whooped Bertie.

He read the label tied round the collar.

**'HI THERE, MY NAME IS TINY!
TRAIN ME TO DO AWESOME TRICKS!
TAKE CARE OF ME AND I'LL BE YOUR BEST BUDDY!**
Warning: keep away from water

This was the best present ever! Better even than the prehistoric dino-poop Darren had given him for his birthday. Think of all the things he could do with a robot! Tiny could keep intruders out of Bertie's bedroom. He'd train him to bark at Miss Boot and to bite Know-All Nick. Wait till his friends heard about this –

he'd be the envy of the whole school!

Whiffer trotted over and sniffed Tiny suspiciously. What kind of dog was this? It didn't even *smell* like a dog!

Suzy folded her arms. "So what does it do then?"

"I have to train him first," replied Bertie, reading the instructions.

He found a switch on Tiny's back and flicked it on.

CLICK! WHIRR, WHIRR!

Tiny stirred into life. His eyes flashed red and his head wagged from side to side. Bertie set him on the ground and grabbed the remote control. He pressed a button.

"Sit, Tiny!" he commanded.

BEEP, BEEP! CLICK, CLICK!

Tiny folded his back legs and sat down.

Dirty Bertie

"Amazing!" gasped Dad.

"Wonderful!" said Mum.

Whiffer looked puzzled. No one ever got this excited when *he* sat down.

"Lie down, Tiny!" said Bertie.

WHIRR, CLICK! Tiny lay down.

Now for the big one, thought Bertie.

"Come, Tiny!" he said, patting his knees. "Come to me!"

CLICK, WHIRR! BEEP, BEEP!

Tiny's little legs began to move and he plodded jerkily across the floor.

"Look! He's doing it – he's walking!" cried Bertie.

"Oh, isn't that sweet?" said Mum.

Whiffer growled. He'd seen quite enough. It was time to put this imposter in his place.

GRRR!

He pounced, pinning Tiny to the floor.

Dirty Bertie

BEEP! WHIRR!

GRRR!

"NO, WHIFFER! BAD BOY!" yelled
Bertie, grabbing him by the collar and
yanking him off.

Whiffer hung his head. What had he
done now?

Bertie opened the back door and
shoved him towards it. "OUT!"

WHAM! The door slammed shut.

Whiffer padded to the window and
watched everyone crowd round the
new dog, smiling and clapping. His ears
drooped. What was going on? One
moment he was Bertie's best friend, the
next he'd been replaced by a flat-faced
mutt who walked like a puppet. Well, he
wasn't taking this lying down. He'd show
that pesky pooch who was top dog!

CHAPTER 2

Next morning, Whiffer lay in wait for the postman. Before long a pile of letters thudded on to the mat.

WOOF! WOOF! He bounded into the hall excitedly.

WHIRR, WHIRR! BEEP, BEEP!

Too late – Tiny had got there first. He scooped up the letters in his mouth and trundled past with red eyes flashing. Whiffer drooped after him into the kitchen.

Tiny stopped beside Dad and wagged his tail.

BEEP! RUFF! RUFF!

Dad looked down. "Well, look at this! Tiny's brought the post! Who's a clever boy?"

He patted the little robot on the head and took the letters.

"I've been training him," said Bertie, proudly. "Roll over, Tiny."

Tiny rolled over.

"I must say he's very well behaved." Mum smiled. "Not like *some* dogs I could mention."

"He does everything I tell him," said Bertie. "Watch this!"

He pressed a green button on the remote control. "Dance, Tiny!"

WHIRR, CLICK! ZOOB, ZIB!

Tinny music blared out and Tiny rocked from side to side performing a cute little dance.

"Oh, that's soooo sweet!" cooed Suzy.

Dad looked up from his letter. "Yes and what's more, he doesn't leave hairs on the sofa."

"Or go crazy when the doorbell goes," said Mum.

"And he won't poo on Mrs Nicely's lawn," said Suzy.

They all turned to look at Whiffer.

WOOF! barked Whiffer. *Finally* someone was paying him some attention! His bowl was empty and he was starving. He picked it up and dropped it at

Dirty Bertie

Dad's feet. Dad went on reading his
letter. Whiffer padded over to Mum. But
she was busy talking to Suzy.

What was the matter with everyone?
He carried his bowl over to Bertie and
plonked it down.

WOOF! he barked, gazing up at
Bertie with big, sad eyes. That usually
did the trick.

"Not now, Whiffer, I'm busy!" sighed
Bertie, fiddling with the remote.

Whiffer stared. What was going on?
His bowl was empty! Wasn't anyone
going to notice?

After lunch, Darren and Eugene came
round to play. Bertie had told them all
about Tiny. He took them out into the
garden to show off some of Tiny's tricks.
Whiffer trailed after them, hoping to play
"Fetch" or "Chew the Slipper". Usually
Darren made a fuss of him, but today he
didn't seem to notice he was there.

"A real robot!" gasped Darren. "You
lucky thing!"

"You could teach him to bring you
breakfast in bed," said Eugene.

"And do your homework."

Mmm, it was a tempting idea, thought Bertie. But the instruction booklet only listed Ten Top Tricks like "Sit", "Fetch" and "Beg". All the same, that was ten more tricks than Whiffer could do. Whiffer was about as obedient as a lemon meringue. The thing about Tiny was you could take him anywhere. He didn't bark, he didn't whine and he didn't run off chasing squirrels. And best of all, Bertie was the only one of his friends who had a Robodog.

"Show us a trick," said Darren.

"Okay," said Bertie. "Tiny, lie down!"

WHIRR! CLICK! CLICK!

Tiny lay down.

"Good boy!" said Bertie. "Tiny, roll over!"

Tiny rolled over.

"Show me how you beg!"

Tiny sat up and raised both paws. His ears flopped pathetically.

"Wicked!" laughed Darren.

"Brilliant!" cried Eugene.

Whiffer watched in disbelief. This was too much!

WOOF! WOOF! He bounded over and began chasing his tail in circles.

"What's up with him?" asked Darren.

Dirty Bertie

Bertie shrugged. "Dunno. He's been acting weird ever since I got Tiny."

Tiny showed them how he could play dead. He did his little dance. He plodded over to a tree and cocked his leg. Darren and Eugene laughed as if it was the funniest thing they'd ever seen. Whiffer stared. This was so unfair! When *he* weed against the gate he got in big trouble!

"And wait till you see this," said Bertie, picking up a stick.

"Fetch, Tiny!" He threw the stick over Tiny's head. Whiffer saw his chance. He might not be able to dance, but no one was faster at fetching sticks. He leaped past Bertie, bounding after the stick.

WOOF! WOOF!

WOO—

Hey! Someone had him by the collar!

"NO, WHIFFER. Leave it!" shouted Bertie.

WHIRR! BEEP! CLICK, CLICK!

Tiny trundled over and picked up the stick in his mouth. He brought it back to Bertie and dropped it at his feet. Bertie patted his head.

"Clever boy! Who's a good boy?"

Whiffer growled. *GRRR!* Call that a stick? He'd show that stuck-up pup how to fetch. He looked around. Ah ha! What about that giant stick propping up the washing line?

He bounded across the lawn and seized the clothes prop in his mouth.

TWANG! The washing line sagged to the ground, dragging Mum's sheets in the mud.

Just at that moment, Mum stuck her head out of the back door.

"Bertie, have you seen my ... ARGHH! Look at my washing! It's filthy!"

"It wasn't me!" said Bertie. "It was Whiffer!"

Whiffer tottered over, carrying the giant pole in his mouth. He dropped it at Mum's feet and wagged his tail, looking pleased with himself.

Mum glared at him. "Bad Boy! Get inside!"

CHAPTER 3

Over the next week, Whiffer's behaviour
only got worse. On Tuesday he left a
puddle on the landing. On Wednesday
he hid a filthy bone in Mum and Dad's
bed. On Thursday he tried to bury Tiny's
remote control in the garden. By Friday
Mum and Dad had had enough. They sat
Bertie down for a serious talk.

Dirty Bertie

"This has got to stop," said Mum.

"It can't go on," sighed Dad.

Bertie looked blank. What were they talking about? He hadn't kept worms in his room for ages – at least not anywhere they'd be found.

"What have I done now?" he asked.

"It's not you, it's Whiffer!" said Dad. "He's driving us crazy!"

"He keeps bringing sticks and bones into the house!" said Mum.

"He weed on the carpet!"

"He follows us everywhere!"

"It's not my fault!" grumbled Bertie.

"He's *your* dog," said Dad. "You're supposed to look after him."

"I do!"

"You don't!" said Mum. "Not since you got Tiny. Who took Whiffer to the park this week? Who fed him? Who cleared up his mess?"

Bertie stared at his feet. Perhaps he had neglected Whiffer a bit, but that was because he had so much to do. Tiny was just a puppy and he still needed training. Besides, it was so much fun.

Mum folded her arms. "I'm sorry, Bertie, but this isn't working. Whiffer's *jealous*."

"JEALOUS?" said Bertie.

"Yes! He doesn't like having another dog around. And you ignoring him only makes it worse!"

"I WON'T ignore him," said Bertie. "I'll look after them both!"

Mum looked at Dad. "All right," she sighed. "We'll give it one more week."

"But Whiffer's got to stop driving us mad," said Dad.

CHAPTER 4

"Whiffer, walkies!"

WOOF! WOOF!

Whiffer flew out of the kitchen and pinned Bertie to the wall. It was ages since they'd gone for walkies. Walkies meant the park and the park meant squirrels.

"Good boy," said Bertie, clipping on his lead. "Tiny's coming too."

Dirty Bertie

Whiffer growled and showed his teeth. *GRRR!* Not that mangy little mongrel!

Bertie opened the front door and Whiffer took off, dragging him down the path. Tiny wobbled along behind, beeping and whirring. *This is great*, thought Bertie. *Me and my dogs, all friends together.*

Dirty Bertie

The park was full of people walking
their dogs. There were tall boxers, yappy
terriers and fluffy poodles. But nobody
else had a dog like Tiny. The other
children crowded around Bertie enviously.

"Wow! Is he yours?" asked a little
curly-haired girl.

"Yes," said Bertie. "He's called Tiny.

Want to see him dance?"

Bertie made Tiny perform every one of his tricks. The crowd gasped and clapped. Whiffer looked away, bored.

"Can he fetch my ball?" asked the little girl.

"He can fetch anything," said Bertie, taking the rubber ball. He sent the ball bouncing across the grass.

"Fetch, Tiny!"

Dirty Bertie

CLICK, CLICK! WHIRR! Tiny set off. But Whiffer had seen the ball too. In a blur of speed, he overtook the robot. Seconds later, he was back, dropping the ball at Bertie's feet and wagging his tail.

"No!" said Bertie. "Whiffer, stay. Let Tiny get this one."

Bertie threw the ball as far as he could. Whiffer forgot all about "Stay" – he was much better at "Fetch". He set off, racing past Tiny to get there first. The ball bounced towards the pond.

DOINK! DOINK! ... PLOP!

"TINY, NO, COME BACK...!" yelled Bertie.

Too late. Whiffer plunged into the water, scattering ducks in all directions. Tiny followed, beetling along behind.

Dirty Bertie

Dirty Bertie

SPLASH!

WHIRR, WHIRR! … BEEP! … BLUB BLUB … BLOOP!

Bubbles rose to the surface.

"TINY!" called Bertie. "TINY?"

Silence.

"He can't swim," said the little girl.

Bertie stared.

A moment later Whiffer arrived like a hurricane on four legs and flattened him on the grass. He was muddy, dripping wet and clutching a rubber ball. He dropped it on the grass and barked excitedly.

WOOF! WOOF!

"No! Ha ha! Get off!" giggled Bertie, as Whiffer licked his face.

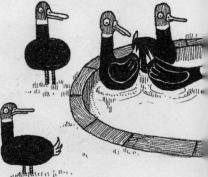

Dirty Bertie

He got up and ruffled Whiffer's fur.
"Good boy," he said. "Tell you what, let's
see if there's any squirrels."

WOOF! Whiffer took off like a furry
bolt of lightning. Bertie ran to catch up.
Tiny had been okay – for a robot – but
there really wasn't anyone like good
old Whiffer!

CHAPTER 1

Bertie opened the front door.

Gran zoomed past him and burst
into the kitchen where Mum, Dad and
Suzy were having tea. Bertie had never
seen her so excited. She looked like
she might take off.

"You'll never guess what!" she panted.
"I'm going to meet the Queen!"

"No!" gasped Mum.

"Yes!"

"Never!"

"I am. Look – here's the invitation!"
She fished in her handbag and
pulled out a silver-trimmed card with
an important-looking coat of arms.

Bertie, Suzy, Mum and Dad crowded
round to look.

Her Majesty The Queen
Graciously Invites

Mrs D. Burns and guest

To a *Royal Garden Party*
at BUCKINGHAM PALACE
Saturday 3rd June

(Please Dress Posh)

"Goodness! A royal garden party?"
said Mum.

"Isn't it exciting?" said Gran. "I can
hardly wait!"

Suzy read the invitation again.

"And guest," she said. "What does
that mean?"

"It means I can bring a friend or
relative," explained Gran.

"What? To meet the Queen?" asked
Bertie, wide-eyed.

"Yes!"

"Actually really MEET her?"

"Yes, actually really."

Bertie could hardly believe his ears.
Imagine that – going to a party at the
Queen's house! Bertie loved parties and
this would be the greatest ever. Think
of the food – royal jelly and king-sized

ice creams. Think of the games – Musical Thrones, Pass the Diamonds and Hide and Seek with a hundred rooms to choose from. Maybe the Queen would decide to knight him? Maybe she'd

even let him borrow her crown for a day to wear to school? Hang on though, didn't Gran say she could only take *one* guest to the party? And she hadn't said who it would be!

"Let me take your coat, Dotty," said Mum, steering Gran into a chair.

"Are you comfy? I'll get you a cushion!" simpered Suzy.

"Have some cake!" offered Dad, cutting a huge slice of sponge.

Bertie scowled. He could see what his sneaky family were up to. They wanted Gran to choose them!

"Well? Have you decided?" asked Mum.

"Decided what?"

"Who you're taking to the garden party?"

"Oh yes," said Gran. She dabbed her lips with a napkin. "Well, it wasn't easy, I've got so many friends. But in the end I thought – who do I know that's never been to London? Who's never even seen Buckingham Palace?"

"ME!" yelled Bertie, banging into the table and spilling the cups.

"BERTIE?" gasped Suzy.

"Is that a good idea?" said Dad. "I mean Bertie – meeting the Queen?"

"Why shouldn't I meet her?" demanded Bertie.

"Well, it's just … sometimes you forget your manners."

"I don't!" said Bertie, grabbing another slice of cake.

Of course there was the time the lady Mayoress visited his school. That was

Dirty Bertie

a bit of a disaster. But it wasn't easy to shake hands with a bogey stuck to your finger. Still, Bertie was sure he wouldn't make the same mistake with the Queen. She probably had servants to deal with that sort of thing.

CHAPTER 2

Bertie couldn't wait to tell his friends at school. They were going to be so jealous! He waited until break time when they were out in the playground.

"What are you doing next Saturday?" he said.

Darren shrugged. "Nothing."

"I've got swimming," said Donna.

Dirty Bertie

"I've got to visit my aunt," said
Eugene, gloomily.

"Oh. Only I won't be here," said
Bertie. "I've got to go to London.
To meet the Queen."

The others stared at him boggle-
eyed. Darren burst out laughing.

"YOU? MEET THE QUEEN? HA HA!"

"Good one, Bertie," grinned Eugene.
"For a minute I almost believed you."

"It's *true!*" said Bertie. "She's giving
a gardening party. Me and Gran are
invited."

"Invited to what?" asked a drawling
voice. Bertie groaned. Trust Know-
All Nick to poke his nose in where it
wasn't wanted!

"Bertie reckons he's going to meet the
Queen," grinned Darren.

Dirty Bertie

"Oh ha ha, very funny," sneered Nick.

"I am!" said Bertie.

"Liar liar, pants on fire!"

"All right, don't believe me," said Bertie, huffily.

"I don't," said Nick.

"Okay, I'll bring you the invitation."

"Huh! Anyone could write an invitation," scoffed Nick. "Prove you met the Queen, then I might believe you."

"Right, I will!" said Bertie. "I'll get her photo. We'll soon see who's lying!"

The week went by slowly. As the big day drew near, Bertie's parents gave him lots of helpful advice.

"Don't mumble!" said Dad.

"Don't slouch!" said Mum.

"And please, please, please DON'T PICK YOUR NOSE!"

"I'm not going to," sighed Bertie. Anyone would think he had no manners at all!

Mum pulled up a chair. "All right, let's have a practice. Pretend I'm the Queen and we've just met. Now, what do you say?"

"Um… Where's the food?" said Bertie.

"You can't ask the Queen that!"

"Why not? I'll be hungry."

"You have to make Polite Conversation," said Mum. "And remember to call her 'Your Majesty'. Now try again. Ahem… Good afternoon, young man."

"Good hafternoon, Your Magicsty," said Bertie.

Mum gave him a look. "Why are you talking like that?"

"I'm makin' polite what-you-said."

"You sound like you've got a mouthful of chewing gum. Speak normally! And stop bobbing up and down!"

"I'm bowing!" said Bertie.

"Well don't! Keep still and talk to me. And hurry up, the Queen hasn't got all day!"

"Good afternoon, Your Magicsty," said Bertie. "Um, when do we eat?"

Mum gave up. There would be hundreds of people at the garden party. With any luck, Bertie wouldn't get within a mile of the Queen. She certainly hoped not.

CHAPTER 3

The great day finally dawned. At ten o'clock on Saturday morning, Bertie knocked on Gran's front door. Gran did a double take. Was this really her grandson? Bertie's face shone, his hair was neatly parted and he was wearing a tie.

"My goodness!" she cried. "I hardly

recognized you. You look as if you've been polished!"

Gran took his picture. Then Bertie took a picture of Gran in her new dress and hat. Then they set off for the station.

Just after two o'clock they presented themselves at the palace gates. A man wearing a smart uniform showed them through to the biggest garden Bertie had ever seen. It had wide green lawns, magnificent fountains and statues with bare bottoms. Across the lawn, hundreds of people were spilling out of an enormous white tent.

Bertie stared. How was he going to meet the Queen with all this lot?

Inside the tent, things didn't get any better. He could hardly move without treading on someone's foot or being poked by a handbag. Bertie sighed. Where was the party food? The royal jelly and ice cream? A waiter passed by with a tray of dainty cucumber sandwiches. Bertie took one and crammed it into his mouth. It would hardly have fed a goldfish.

He looked around. This was going to be the worst party ever. Everyone was nearly as old as Gran – and all they did was stand around talking and sipping tea. Worst of all, the Queen hadn't even bothered to turn up! Bertie had been keeping an eye out for someone wearing a sparkly gold crown, but there was no sign of her. At this rate he would never get a photo. What would he tell all his friends?

Dirty Bertie

Dirty Bertie

"BERTIE!" hissed Gran.

"What?"

"Don't eat so fast. And don't say 'what?' say 'pardon'."

"But I didn't burp!" protested Bertie. He sighed. "Can I see if there's any cake?"

Gran rolled her eyes. "If you must. But don't be greedy."

Bertie pushed his way through the crowd until he spotted a waiter with a plate of cakes. There were dainty cupcakes, macaroons and lemon slices. He tugged on the waiter's sleeve, and started to fill his plate. A voice interrupted him.

"Are you having a nice time?"

Bertie turned to see a lady in a pale blue dress, with a matching hat. She was about Gran's age, but spoke terribly nicely, as if she was reading the news.

"Er, yes … yes thanks," said Bertie.

"One imagines this might not be your cup of tea," said the smiling lady.

"Oh, I don't drink tea," said Bertie. "I tried it once but I spat it out."

"I meant the garden party. Are you really having a nice time?"

"Honestly?" said Bertie, cramming a cupcake into his mouth.

"Honestly."

Dirty Bertie

Bertie lowered his voice. "It's dead boring. There's nothing to do."

"Ah," said the lady. "I see."

"I mean look!" said Bertie, spraying cake crumbs everywhere. "You'd think the Queen'd do better than this. There aren't even any balloons or games! She could at least have got a bouncy castle!"

The lady seemed to find this idea amusing. "People would have to take off their hats," she said.

Bertie caught sight of Gran, who seemed to be trying to tell him something. She pointed at Bertie's companion and waved her hands as if she was swatting flies. Bertie hadn't a clue what she meant. He'd only taken four cakes so he was hardly being greedy.

Other people were waiting to meet the lady in the blue hat. She seemed surprisingly popular.

"Well, I enjoyed our little chat," she said. "Tell me, are you fond of dogs?"

"Um, yes, I've got a dog," said Bertie. "He's called Whiffer."

"I have corgis. Five. Molly, Polly, Vicky, Georgia and Jemima. Perhaps you'd like to see them?"

"Me?" said Bertie.

"Yes, my footman will show you the way."

A man in a black uniform bowed. Bertie wondered why the lady had a footman. Maybe she had bad feet? In any case, dogs were much more interesting than people. He followed the footman out of the tent to a small courtyard. A maid stood waiting with five fat little corgis, all pulling on their leads.

CHAPTER 4

Bertie let the corgis lick the cake crumbs off his hand.

"You like dogs?" asked the maid.

"Yes," replied Bertie. "Do you?"

"Can't stand 'em. Smelly, yappy things. Want to hold them for a bit?"

"Can I?"

Bertie took the leads from the maid,

who seemed glad of a break. Molly,
Polly, Vicky, Georgia and Jemima sniffed
round his legs.

"They haven't had their walkies yet,"
said the maid.

"I could take them," said Bertie. "I'm
not doing anything."

The maid considered. "Okay, just
round the gardens. But keep 'em on
the lead."

Bertie set off. He was used to taking
Whiffer for walks, but five excited corgis
were a lot more trouble. They pulled in
different directions and their leads got
tangled under his feet. They crossed the
lawn, passing the Queen's garden party.
Ooops! Bertie stumbled over a tap.

WHOOSH! A garden sprinkler came
on, spraying him with jets of water.

"Arghh! Oooh!" yelped Bertie,
letting go of the dog leads.

Free at last, the corgis bolted
through a flower bed and raced across
the lawn.

"NO! COME BACK!" yelled Bertie,
as they headed for the door of the big
white tent.

He chased after them. The party was still in full flow, but as he reached the tent he heard a terrible noise.

WOOF! CRASH! TINKLE! THUNK!

Bertie barged his way through the crowd. He stared in horror. A waiter was lying on the floor, surrounded by broken cups and plates. Five fat little corgis were clambering over him, licking up cream and bits of cupcake.

"Crumbs!" gasped Bertie.

Dirty Bertie

The party had fallen silent. The waiter scrambled to his feet and bowed to the lady in the blue hat.

"Your Majesty, I'm most terribly sorry," he said.

Dirty Bertie

Bertie gaped. "Your *Majesty?*"
Then the lady in the blue hat was the
QUEEN? Why hadn't anyone warned
him? He'd told her that her party was
boring. He'd let her dogs loose and
broken her best plates. She would
probably have his head chopped off!

The Queen turned to Bertie and
raised her eyebrows.

"Ah," she said. "And what
do you have to say for
yourself?"

Bertie gulped. He bowed
low.

"Your Magicsty ... um,
would you be in a
photo?"

Dirty Bertie

The following Monday, Bertie's friends were waiting for him in the playground. They hadn't forgotten his ridiculous boast.

"So?" grinned Darren. "How was the party?"

"Did you see the palace?" asked Eugene.

"And did you meet Her Majesty?" jeered Know-All Nick.

Bertie waited for them to stop laughing. "Actually, I did," he said. "We had a good chat."

"Liar!" snorted Nick. "You're making it up."

"Am I," said Bertie. He reached into his pocket and brought out a photo.

Nick stared. His mouth fell open. He turned white, then green.

"You can keep it if you like," said Bertie. "I've got lots!"

WEDDING!

CHAPTER 1

Bertie groaned.

"It's not fair! Why do I have to go?"

"It's your cousin's wedding," said Mum.

"I love weddings," sighed Suzy. "So romantic!"

"Yuck! I hate them!" said Bertie.

The last wedding his parents had dragged him to was deathly dull. He had

to sit through speeches that went on
for days. Even when it was time to leave
there were armies of aunts waiting to
kiss him. This time, his cousin Dora was
marrying her fiancé, Bruce. Bertie had
met drippy Dora. He couldn't see why
anyone would want to talk to her – let
alone marry her.

"In any case, we're going," said
Mum. "Suzy's a bridesmaid and you're
a pageboy."

Bertie looked horrified. *Him*? A
pageboy?

"No way!" he cried.

"All you have to do is look smart,"
said Mum.

"I *never* look smart," said Bertie,
truthfully.

"You will for Dora's wedding," said

Mum firmly. "That's why I'm taking you shopping on Saturday. Suzy can find a bridesmaid's dress and we'll get you a kilt."

"A KILT?" Bertie gasped for air. "But that's a ... a..."

"A SKIRT!" giggled Suzy. "HA HA!"

"Don't be silly," said Mum. "Bruce is Scottish and lots of the men will be wearing kilts."

"But can't I just wear jeans?" begged Bertie.

"Of course not! It's a wedding!"

Bertie groaned. This was torture! Cruelty! It couldn't be happening!

Dirty Bertie

On Saturday morning Mum took them
to "Gladrags" wedding shop in town. The
snooty assistant helped them to choose
things to try on. Suzy picked a pretty
lilac dress with puff sleeves and went to
change. Bertie didn't choose anything. The
kilts were all too big, too baggy, too …
skirty! In the end Mum chose one for him.
Bertie took it into the changing room and
slammed the door.

A moment later, Suzy appeared.

"Oh darling, you look lovely!" said
Mum.

Suzy twirled round in front of the
mirror. She'd always dreamed of being
a bridesmaid. It was just a pity Bertie
would be there to spoil the pictures.

"Where is Bertie?" Mum frowned.
"He's been in there ages."

She knocked on the changing room
door. "BERTIE?"

"He's not here!"

"Bertie, hurry up, we're waiting!"

Dirty Bertie

"It doesn't fit. It's too big!" grumbled Bertie.

"Nonsense! Let me see!" said Mum.

"NO!"

Mum folded her arms. "Right, I'm counting to three. One, two, thr—"

BLAM! The door burst open. Bertie stomped out, scowling furiously. He was wearing a black jacket, a frilly shirt and a green kilt with a hairy sporran. It was the smallest kilt in the shop, but it practically reached Bertie's ankles.

"It's too big!" he moaned. "I look stupid!"

"Ahh," said Suzy. "Do you want an ickle pink bow for your hair?"

"SHUT UP!" cried Bertie.

"Take no notice," said Mum. "Lots of boys wear kilts. I think you look very handsome."

Bertie scowled at his reflection in the mirror. Handsome? He couldn't go out like this! What if one of his friends saw him? It was bad enough that he had to be at Dora's wedding, but dressed in a tartan skirt? No, he wouldn't do it, not for his cousin, not for anyone. And there was nothing they could do to make him.

CHAPTER 2

Bertie climbed into the car and slumped
on the back seat. It was the morning
of Bruce and Dora's wedding. He had
tried everything to get out of wearing
the horrible hairy kilt. First he'd claimed
it was torn, then lost, then that it'd fallen
down the toilet. Mum wasn't fooled.
She said he was wearing the kilt and

he'd better get used to it.

The cars set off for the church. Bertie was going with Suzy and Neil, the best man. Bertie wriggled around. His kilt was itchy. He tucked it between his legs. He hoped it wasn't a windy day. Dad said that Scots didn't wear anything under their kilts — but he wasn't falling for that one! He was wearing two pairs of pants, just in case.

"Move over!" grumbled Suzy.

"You move over!" said Bertie.

"No! You're creasing my dress!"

Neil groaned. "Stop squabbling! You're giving me a headache!"

Bertie rolled his eyes. What a fusspot! If Bertie ever needed a best man it wouldn't be Neil.

Neil looked at his watch. He checked

he had his hanky and his speech.
He checked he'd got the ring in the
little box.

"What's that?" asked Bertie.

"The wedding ring, stupid," said Suzy.

"Can I see it?"

"Certainly not!" said Neil.

"Please. Please, please, please…"

"Oh all right," groaned Neil. "Just be careful!"

Bertie opened the box. "Wow!" he
gasped. "Is it real gold?"

"Of course it's real!"

Bertie had never actually held
a real gold ring. The only rings he
ever got were out of Christmas crackers.
Dora must have small hands because this
ring was tiny. Bertie held it up. Maybe
it would fit him? He slipped it over his

thumb to see.

"BERTIE!" snapped Neil. "Give it back."

"Okay, okay," sighed Bertie. Some people were so impatient!

He pulled at the ring. Oops! It wouldn't come off. He tried to twist it. Argh! He tugged. He wrestled and wriggled. It wouldn't budge.

"Bertie, come ON!" groaned Neil.

"I'm … trying!" panted Bertie. "It seems to be … arrrr … stuck!"

The car turned a corner and pulled up outside the church. They all climbed out. In desperation Neil and Suzy took it in turns to try and pull the ring off Bertie's thumb.

"Keep still!"

"I am ... OW! That hurts!" moaned Bertie.

It was no use. The ring was stuck like superglue. No matter how much they pulled and yanked, it wouldn't come off. A car drew up and Mum and Dad got out.

"Everything okay?" said Dad.

"It's Bertie," said Suzy. "He was playing with the ring and now he's got it stuck!"

"What?"

Bertie held up his thumb to show them.

Dirty Bertie

"It's not my fault!" he grumbled. "How was I to know it wouldn't come off?"

"Of course it's your fault," cried Neil. "You should never have touched it in the first place."

He paced up and down in a panic. This was terrible, a nightmare! Everyone was in the church waiting, and any minute now Dora would be here. But how could they start the service without a ring?

Dad checked his watch. "What are we going to do?"

Mum had an idea. "Butter!" she cried.

"What?"

"Butter – that's how you get it off! Rub his thumb with butter."

"We don't have any butter!" groaned Neil.

"What about the church hall?" said Suzy.

"Of course!" said Mum. Everyone was going to the church hall after the service for the wedding party. There would be stacks of food. They were bound to find butter somewhere.

Just then, a big white car drew up outside the church. The bride had arrived. Dora got out, trailing vast clouds of silk. Mum sprang into action.

Dirty Bertie

"Quick," she said. "I'll try to delay them. Bertie, run to the hall with Dad."

"Me? What for?" said Bertie.

"To find some butter!" cried Mum. "And for heaven's sake, HURRY!"

CHAPTER 3

Bertie and Dad ran to the church hall.
It was empty. The room was set out with
chairs and tables ready for the wedding
party. At the far end was a long table
with drinks and nibbles for the guests.
Bertie's eyes lit up. He hadn't eaten
anything since breakfast.

"Right," said Dad. "You look in here,

Dirty Bertie

Bertie. I'll try the kitchen."

Dad hurried off. Bertie gazed hungrily at the nibbles. He helped himself to a handful of crisps, just to help him think. What had Mum said? Oh yes, butter. Where did they keep the butter? He searched the table. Peanuts, dips, sausage rolls – but no butter.

"Find any?" shouted Dad, clattering cupboard doors in the kitchen.

"No, not yet!"

Bertie grabbed some more crisps in case the service went on a bit. Luckily his sporran was the perfect place to keep a snack. He checked to see Dad wasn't watching. Wait, what was this? Bruce and Dora's

wedding cake was sitting on a trolley.
Bertie loved cake, and this one was
a monster. It was a three cake tower
trimmed with pink roses. On the bottom
cake, written in icing, it said:

Congrats on Your
Wonderful Day

Bertie stared. Icing – of course! Icing was just like butter. His finger hovered over the beautiful wedding cake. Should he? Time was running out and he had to get the ring off. This was his last chance. SHHLUPP! Bertie scooped up a big splodge of icing.

Mmm – not bad! He tried a pink rose. *Mmm mmm mmm.*

Remembering his mum's advice, he slathered his thumb in icing and licked it off. Whoops! The writing on the cake had got a bit smudged. Some of the letters were missing. But what about the ring? He twisted it. YES! It slid over his thumb. Genius!

"Any luck, Bertie?" cried Dad, suddenly appearing from the kitchen.

Bertie stood in front of the cake.

"Oh ... um, yes. Look, I got it off!"

He held up the ring triumphantly.

"Thank goodness!" said Dad. "You found some butter?"

"Er, sort of," said Bertie.

"Then what are we standing here for?" said Dad. "Let's get back to the church!"

Bertie glanced over his shoulder at the cake as he left. It did look a bit messy. But it was too late to do anything about it now. After all, it was only a cake. Who was going to notice?

CHAPTER 4

They reached the church and stood
outside, panting for breath. Dad put
his ear to the door. He groaned.

"They've already started!"

"What?" cried Bertie. "They can't
have!"

"They obviously couldn't wait! We'll
have to sneak in quietly," said Dad.

"But what about the ring?" said Bertie, holding it up.

"Give it to Neil! Just try not to draw attention to yourself."

Inside the church, Dora and Bruce stood at the altar. The vicar was reaching the part with the wedding vows. Neil wiped a drop of sweat from his forehead. Where in the name of heaven was Bertie? If he didn't get here soon it would be too late!

"Dora Lara Spooner," said the vicar, "do you take this man to be your husband?"

"I do," trilled Dora.

"Bruce John McDougal, do you take this woman to be your wife?"

"I do," boomed Bruce.

There was a long pause.

"The ring!" whispered the vicar.

"Oh, um, yes, the ring…" stammered Neil, turning bright pink. He searched his pockets as if that might help.

"Neil!" hissed Dora.

Neil shook his head helplessly. "I … er … I haven't…"

Dirty Bertie

CRASH!

Every head in the church turned round to look. Bertie had zoomed up the aisle and skidded, falling flat on his face. His kilt had flopped over, so everyone got a good view of his pants. Suzy giggled.

"BERTIE!" hissed Neil.

Bertie got up. He pulled down his kilt and came forward. In his hand was something pink and sticky like a half-sucked sweet. He handed it over. Bruce slid the ring over Dora's finger.

"EUGH!" said Dora.

After the service they all crowded into the church hall for the wedding party. Bertie had to sit through hours of boring speeches, but he didn't care. He was off the hook. Dora grumbled that he'd almost ruined her big day, but Bruce patted his head and said no harm was done.

Neil stood up and banged on the table with a spoon.

"And now, the bride and groom will cut the cake!"

Dirty Bertie

Bertie gulped. Oh no! The cake – he'd forgotten all about it!

A lady pushed the trolley to the front where the bride and groom stood waiting. Dora took the knife ready to cut the first slice. She stared. She gasped. She looked like she might faint.

Her beautiful wedding cake – ruined! The tower was looking wonky, and there were sticky fingermarks all over it. Someone had scoffed most of the pink roses. Worst of all, the message was missing some letters, so now it read:

Dirty Bertie

"EEEK! MY CAKE!" shrieked Dora.

Mum and Dad turned round. There was only one person who could have done this, and he was wearing a sticky kilt and a guilty expression.

"BERTIE!" groaned Mum.

Bertie gulped. He put his hand into his sporran.

"Um … anyone want a crisp?"

Dirty Bertie

KISS!

For the lovely Lauren Ace ~ D R

For Ted – may you always have a BFF ~ A M

Contents

CHAPTER 1

It was morning break. Bertie reached
into his pocket for his secret weapon:
a slimy slug. Unlike most people, Bertie
liked slugs. He liked their sluggy colour
and the cold, slippery feel of them.
He looked around the playground.
Who would be his first victim? Royston
Rich? Royston was always bragging that

nothing scared him. Or Know-All Nick? Bertie would enjoy putting a slug down his neck. But Nick would only tell tales to Miss Boot. He had a better idea – what about Angela Nicely? Angela lived next door to Bertie and she'd been in love with him for ever. She was always telling people that he was her boyfriend. Well, he'd soon put a stop to that. Wait till Angela saw the fat, slimy slug he'd got for her. How she'd scream and beg for mercy!

♥   ♥   ♥

Angela was sitting on a bench, playing a game with her friends, Laura and Maisie.

"Your go, Laura," said Maisie. "Truth, Dare, Kiss or Promise?"

"Truth," said Laura.

Dirty Bertie

"Is it true … I'm your Best Friend Forever?" said Maisie.

Laura thought hard. "No," she said. "Angela is."

Maisie sulked.

"My go, my go!" sang Angela, excitedly.

"Okay," said Laura. "Truth, Dare, Kiss or Promise?"

Angela smiled. "KISS!" she said.

"ANGELA!" squealed Laura and Maisie. "You'll have to kiss a boy!"

"I don't care!" declared Angela.

"All right, but you've got to kiss whoever we say," said Maisie.

"That's the rules," agreed Laura. "Or else you're out of the game."

Maisie looked around the playground for a likely victim. It had to be someone disgusting – some grubby, bogey-nosed boy.

"OH, ANG-ELA!" yelled Bertie, holding up the slug. "Look what I've got!"

Maisie grinned. "HIM!" she said, pointing.

"Yes, Bertie, kiss Bertie!" cried Laura.

Bertie turned pale. His mouth fell open. "W-what?"

"ANGELA WANTS TO KISS YOU!" chanted the girls.

"No she doesn't!" gasped Bertie.

"Yes I do!" beamed Angela, jumping to her feet. "I've got to. It's the rules!"

Bertie turned pink. He backed away. What rules? Had they all gone mad?

"Keep back!" he cried. "I've got a slug!"

"I don't care!" said Angela, coming closer.

"A big wet, slimy slug," said Bertie, holding it out. "I'll put it in your hair!"

But Angela just kept coming. "I'm going to kiss you!" she sang.

"No!" gasped Bertie.

"Yes I am!"

Dirty Bertie

"Go on, Angela!" urged Laura.

"Keep back!" yelled Bertie, desperately.
"Don't come near me!"

Angela took no notice. She puckered
her lips and leaned in closer.

"ARGHHHHHHH!" yelled Bertie.
He dropped the slug and ran for it.

CHAPTER 2

Darren and Eugene were sitting on the wall at the far end of the playground.

"Quick!" panted Bertie, tearing round the corner. "Help me hide!"

"What's going on?" asked Darren.

"She's after me!"

"Who? Miss Boot?"

"No! Angela!"

Dirty Bertie

They both stared at him. "Angela?" said Eugene. "Angela in Class 1?"

"You don't understand," said Bertie. "She wants to…" He could hardly bring himself to say it. "She wants to *kiss* me!"

"KISS YOU!" howled Darren and Eugene.

"Shh! Don't tell everyone!" groaned Bertie.

"But *kiss* you! Ha ha! Hee hee!" chortled his friends, helpless with laughter.

Dirty Bertie

"It's not funny!" groaned Bertie. "She won't leave me alone! Don't let her find me!"

"You better hide then," grinned Darren. "Here she comes."

Bertie dived behind a tub of flowers. A moment later, Angela and her friends came running up.

"Have you seen Bertie?" asked Angela, breathlessly.

Darren looked at Eugene. "Let me think ... have we seen Bertie?"

Eugene frowned. "I don't think so."

"Why do you want him?" asked Darren.

Angela beamed. "I'm going to kiss him!"

"It's the rules!" Laura explained. "She has to, don't you, Angela?"

Angela nodded. She didn't mind kissing Bertie. After all, he was her boyfriend.

"Oh, *you're* Angela," said Darren. "Bertie's always talking about you, isn't he, Eugene?"

"Er … yeah," said Eugene. "He loves you."

"He wants to marry you!" said Darren.

Angela stared. "Really? He said that?"

"Millions of times," said Darren. "But you know what he'd like best?"

Angela shook her head.

"A big fat kiss!" said Darren.

Angela clapped her hands. "I'm going to!" she said. "I'm going to kiss him as soon as I find him! Come on!"

She ran off, with her two friends chasing behind.

"Ha ha! Hee hee!" hooted Darren and Eugene, holding their sides.

Bertie crept out from his hiding place. "What did you tell her that for? Now she thinks I like her!"

"No," grinned Darren. "She thinks you LOVE her."

"And you want to marry her!" said Eugene.

Bertie held his head. "Stop saying that! I DON'T!"

"Yes, you *do*! Bertie loves Angela!

Dirty Bertie

Bertie loves Angela!" chanted Darren
and Eugene.

"SHUT UP!" yelled Bertie. What if
people heard? This was growing worse
by the minute.

"Look! There he is!" cried a shrill
voice. "BERTIE!"

Bertie turned. *Help!* Angela had
spotted him. *RUN!*

♥   ♥   ♥

Bertie screeched round a corner and
ducked into the boys' toilets. He darted
into one of the cubicles, locking the
door behind him. *Phew! Made it!* Angela
and her friends had chased him all over
the playground – but they couldn't
follow him in here. He slumped against
the wall, his heart beating fast.

Dirty Bertie

This is a nightmare, he thought. *What
if she catches me?* Angela was only small,
but she was extremely determined.
Imagine it – Bertie, the Terror of Class
3, kissed by a girl. YUCK! It was too
horrible for words. He'd never be able to
show his face again.

CREAK!

The door of the boys' toilets opened.
Bertie froze in terror. Surely it couldn't
be Angela?

Footsteps crossed the floor.

CLUMP! CLUMP!
CLUMP!

They stopped
right outside his
door. Bertie held
his breath.

RATTLE! RATTLE!

Someone tried the door handle. Bertie shrank back against the wall.

"BERTIE!" boomed a voice. "I KNOW YOU'RE IN THERE!"

Bertie sagged with relief. Even facing the wrath of Miss Boot was better than being kissed by Angela!

"Just going to the toilet, Miss!" he called.

"Well, get a move on. The bell went five minutes ago!"

CHAPTER 3

Back in class, Bertie tried to stay calm. Angela couldn't get him here. He was safe until lunchtime, and by then she might have forgotten the whole thing. He leaned over and tried to sneak a look at Eugene's answer sheet.

"BERTIE!"

He looked up. Miss Boot was

beckoning him forward.

"Uh oh, trouble," murmured Darren.

Bertie trailed out to the front. What had he done this time? Miss Boot pointed to a pile of books on her desk.

"Take these to Miss Darling," she said.

Bertie brightened up – anything was better than maths. But wait a minute, didn't Miss Darling teach Class 1? That was Angela's class!

"Can't someone else go?" he begged. "I've got a bad leg."

"You were fine just now," snapped Miss Boot.

"But Miss…"

"No arguments, Bertie. And make sure you come straight back."

Huh! He certainly wouldn't be hanging around – not if Angela was nearby.

Dirty Bertie

♥   ♥   ♥

Five minutes later he knocked on the
door of Class 1.

"Come in!" called Miss Darling.

Bertie tottered in, trying not to drop
the books.

"Miss Boot said to bring you these."

"Thank you, Bertie." Miss Darling
smiled. "Put them in the storeroom,
can you?"

But Bertie wasn't listening. Someone
at the back of the class
was waving to him.
Angela Nicely. Bertie
felt hot. He
thought he
might
pass out.

"Are you all right?" asked Miss Darling. "The books, Bertie. Put them away."

"Oh yes, right." Bertie hurried over to the storeroom. Inside he flicked on the light. Rows of shelves were stacked with hundreds of books.

CLICK!

He spun round. Someone had come in, and shut the door. *Help!* Angela and her friends. Bertie backed towards the shelves. He was trapped!

"Hello, Bertie!" smiled Angela.

"Keep back!" warned Bertie.

"It's your girlfriend," said Maisie. "She just wants one little kiss."

"BLECH!" said Bertie.

"You love her," said Laura. "You want to marry her!"

"I'd rather marry a slug!" replied Bertie.

Dirty Bertie

Angela kept coming – insults had no effect.

"Stay back or I'll … I'll burp!" threatened Bertie.

"I don't care!" said Angela. "I'm going to kiss you!"

Bertie looked around for some kind of weapon. There was nothing but books. He jumped on to a chair. Angela grabbed him round the legs. She pulled. Bertie wobbled. The chair tipped and he lost his balance.

"ARGHHHH!"

THUD! BANG! THUMP!

Bertie sprawled on the floor under a pile of books. The storeroom door flew open and Miss Darling appeared.

"What's going on in here?" she cried, glaring at the three girls.

"Angela, I'm surprised at you! Are you meant to be in here?"

Angela hung her head. "No, Miss."

"Then get back to your work. And Bertie, clear up this mess and return to your class."

"Yes, Miss. Thank you, Miss," said Bertie, gratefully. He picked himself up. It had been a close call, but he had survived.

CHAPTER 4

Bertie checked the clock. It had been a long day. Every time he turned a corner, Angela seemed to be lying in wait. At lunch-break he'd avoided her by staying close to Miss Boot. But now it was almost home time. Angela and her friends would be waiting for him outside. His only chance was to make a quick getaway.

Dirty Bertie

DRRINGGG!

The bell went. Bertie shot out of his place. He streaked for the door like a greyhound.

"BERTIE!" barked Miss Boot. "WHERE DO YOU THINK YOU'RE GOING?"

"Home, Miss."

"Did I say you could go?"

"No, but—"

"Then sit down and wait till you're told."

Darren and Eugene grinned as Bertie drooped back to his seat. Miss Boot droned on about homework. By the time she finished it was too late. Through the window, Bertie could see Angela and her pals guarding the gates.

He slunk into the cloakroom and hid behind the coat racks.

"What are you doing?" asked Eugene.

"Hiding. From Angela!" hissed Bertie.

"Your girlfriend?" said Darren.

"It's not funny!" grumbled Bertie. "You should help me, instead of making stupid jokes."

"I'd like to," said Darren, "but I've got to get back. Mum's getting me new trainers. Tell you what, I'll come round later to check you made it home alive," he said.

Eugene hung back. "Are you coming, Bertie?"

"I can't," said Bertie. "She'll see me!"

"Not if you sneak past her," said Eugene. "You could wear a disguise."

A *disguise*, thought Bertie – it wasn't

such a bad idea. But what? He looked around. Someone had left a coat hanging on one of the pegs. He tried it on. He was only going to borrow it ... after all, this was an emergency.

♥   ♥   ♥

Five minutes later, Eugene and Bertie crossed the playground. Bertie's face was hidden by a bright pink anorak. He felt ridiculous.

"This had better work," he whispered.

"It will, trust me," said Eugene. "Just don't say a word."

They reached the gates. Angela and her pals blocked their path.

"Have you seen Bertie?" asked Angela.

"Er, no," said Eugene. "He must've gone home."

Dirty Bertie

Angela shook her head. "He hasn't come out yet. We've been watching." She stared at the girl in the pink anorak. "Have *you* seen him?"

Bertie shook his head, keeping it lowered.

"She's a bit shy," explained Eugene.

"What's her name?"

"Er … Tina," said Eugene.

Dirty Bertie

"I'm Angela," said Angela. "When Bertie comes out I'm going to kiss him."

"No chance," muttered Bertie.

"Pardon?"

"She said, 'Oh pants, we'd better go!'" replied Eugene. "Come on, Tina!"

Angela watched them hurry past. She noticed Tina was wearing muddy trainers – just like Bertie's. Come to think of it, she walked like Bertie too. Angela ran after her and pulled down her hood.

"BERTIE!" she squawked.

"Quick!" yelled Bertie. "RUN!"

Dirty Bertie

♥ ♥ ♥

Back home, Bertie leaned against the front door, panting for breath. Angela would have caught him this time, if he hadn't been too fast for her. He thumped upstairs and threw himself on his bed. No way was any girl going to kiss him. They'd have to catch him first, and he was way too clever. Bertie smiled to himself as he reached for his secret stash of biscuits.

He was munching the last one when the doorbell rang.

"Bertie, it's for you!" yelled his sister, Suzy. "It's one of your friends!"

"Send them up," shouted Bertie. It was probably Darren come to make fun of him. Ha! Wait till he told him about his brilliant escape.

Dirty Bertie

The door opened. Bertie looked up.
"Hello, Bertie!" beamed Angela. "All
on your own?"

CHAPTER 1

Bertie yawned and glanced at the clock.
Ten minutes to go. Tomorrow was the
start of the half-term holidays.

Over by the window Snuffles, the
class hamster, dozed in his cage. Snuffles
was a legend. Miss Boot said he was six
years old, which for a hamster was like
a hundred or something. If he lived much

longer he'd probably make it into the *Guinness World Records*. It was just a pity he slept so much of the time. Bertie reckoned it was because he was bored. Anyone would be bored having to listen to Miss Boot every day. If Snuffles was Bertie's pet he would have taught him tricks – rolling over, standing on his head, maybe even tightrope walking.

Dirty Bertie

Bertie sighed. It was pointless even thinking about it – Miss Boot would never trust him with Snuffles. Over the holidays the class took it in turns to look after the hamster, but Miss Boot only chose "sensible" children. She had pinned a list of names on the wall. Eugene was on the list, so was Donna and Know-All Nick. Bertie wasn't. It wasn't fair. Why did he never get picked for anything?

DRRINGGG!

The bell rang for home time. Everyone cheered and packed away their books.

"Wait!" boomed Miss Boot. "Who is taking Snuffles home for the holidays?"

Donna raised her hand. "It's Eugene's turn, Miss."

"Ah, yes," said Miss Boot. "Wait behind please, Eugene."

Dirty Bertie

The class piled out of the door. Bertie waited with Eugene while Miss Boot collected together Snuffles' things.

"Don't forget to clean out his cage and give him food and water every day," said Miss Boot.

"Yes… Oh no!" Eugene gasped.

"What's the matter?" asked Miss Boot.

"I just remembered – we're away this week visiting my gran."

Miss Boot rolled her eyes. "Isn't anyone staying at home?"

Eugene shook his head.

"Really! Why didn't you say so before?" asked Miss Boot.

"I forgot," said Eugene.

"Well, who's going to look after Snuffles? We can't leave him here – and everyone's gone home."

Dirty Bertie

"I haven't!" said Bertie, eagerly.

Miss Boot glared. "*You?*"

"Yes, I could look after him."

"But you haven't asked your parents," said Miss Boot. "What if they say no?"

"They won't," Bertie replied. "My mum loves pets!"

This wasn't strictly true, but Bertie wasn't going to let a little thing like that get in the way. This might be his only chance to look after Snuffles.

"Please!" he begged.

Miss Boot groaned. Why Bertie, of all people?

"Very well," she said. "But I am trusting you, Bertie. I've had Snuffles a long time and if anything happened to him I'd be very upset. *Very* upset."

"I'll guard him with my life, Miss," promised Bertie.

"Mind you do," said Miss Boot.

Bertie hurried out, before his teacher changed her mind. At last! Snuffles was his — for a whole week!

CHAPTER 2

CREAK, CREAK, CREAK!

Bertie crept up the stairs, carrying the hamster cage. Now that he'd got Snuffles home, he was beginning to worry. What if Miss Boot was right? What if his mum said no?

"Bertie?" called Mum. "Is that you?"

Uh oh. Bertie turned round, hiding the

cage behind his back. Mum was at the bottom of the stairs.

"What are you doing?" she demanded.

"Nothing. Just going to my room."

Mum narrowed her eyes. "What's that you've got?"

"Where?"

"Behind your back. I'm not blind, Bertie."

"Just … school stuff."

"Show me," said Mum.

Bertie swallowed hard. There was no escape. He brought out the cage and removed the jumper covering it.

Mum groaned. "Bertie! Is that a HAMSTER?"

"No!" said Bertie. "Well, only a little one."

"Where on earth did you get it?"

"From school," Bertie replied. "I was

specially chosen to look after him."

Mum folded her arms. "I told you no more pets," she said. "Whiffer's quite enough trouble."

"But a hamster's different," argued Bertie. "He won't be any trouble."

"No, because we're not keeping him," said Mum.

"Please! It's only for a week."

"No! He'll have to go back."

Dirty Bertie

"He can't! School's closed. If I don't keep him, he's got nowhere to go."

Snuffles gazed up at them with large, sad eyes.

Mum sighed heavily. "All right! But just for a week!"

"Yesssssss!" cried Bertie.

"But he stays in your bedroom," said Mum. "And it's your job to look after him."

"I will!" promised Bertie.

"And don't let him out of his cage."

Bertie gaped. "He'll have to come out sometimes. He needs exercise!"

"We've got a dog!" said Mum. "What happens if Whiffer gets hold of him? I'm not phoning Miss Boot to say her hamster's been eaten!"

Bertie sighed. "Okay, I'll be careful."

He carried the cage up to his room, shutting the door on Whiffer, who was eager to see what was inside.

He'd keep Snuffles in his cage ... at least most of the time. He would only let him out for something important – like learning tricks for instance.

CHAPTER 3

Bertie was eager to get started, but he soon found out that hamsters weren't as much fun as he'd expected.

He began by drawing up a list of tricks to work on. Next he made an obstacle course out of toilet roll tubes and biscuit tins. But Snuffles slept all day and showed no interest. Bertie tried to tempt him out with bits of carrot.

Next day he tried to train Snuffles to balance on top of a ball. Snuffles fell off.

Suzy said he was wasting his time. "Hamsters are nocturnal," she said, "they only come out at night."

Bertie soon discovered this for himself. Snuffles kept him awake every night running round in his wheel. On top of that, Bertie had to keep his door closed, because Whiffer was always whining and trying to get in. By Sunday evening, he was exhausted. Hamsters were so much work!

"Have you cleaned out Snuffles' cage today?" asked Mum, over supper.

Dirty Bertie

"Yes!" groaned Bertie.

"Well, it's dirty again! He does his business in there!"

"EWW! GROSS!" cried Suzy, pulling a face.

"It's only poo," said Bertie. "You can see them in the cage, they're like tiny black sausages…"

"MUM, tell him!" cried Suzy, putting down her fork.

Mum rolled her eyes. "Bertie, please! We're trying to eat!"

"I was only saying," grumbled Bertie.

"Well, never mind the details," said Dad. "Just clean out his cage."

"Can't I do it in the morning?"

"No," said Mum, firmly. "I want that cage spotless tonight."

After supper, Bertie stomped upstairs. *It's not fair*, he thought. *People have to clean up their own poo, so why can't hamsters?* He opened the cage door. Snuffles was awake. He darted around, getting in the way. Bertie took him out and carried him over to his beanbag.

Dirty Bertie

Snuffles crawled around, glad to be free at last.

"You stay there," Bertie told him. "This won't take long."

Ten minutes later, the cage was done. Bertie turned round to get Snuffles.

Yikes! Where did he go?

Dirty Bertie

Bertie grabbed the beanbag but there were no hamsters underneath. He looked around, starting to panic. *Keep calm*, he thought. *He can't have gone far.* He looked under the bed. Nothing. Nothing behind the curtains or the bookcase, either. Bertie turned round.

ARGHHHHH! The bedroom door was open! Snuffles could have wandered out. He could be anywhere!

"Bertie!" called Mum. "Have you finished doing that cage?"

"Um … almost!" Bertie shouted.

"Well, as soon as you have, can you bring me your dirty washing?"

"Okay!" Bertie slumped on to his beanbag. What on earth was he going to do? Mum would go bananas if she found out. He wouldn't tell her – not yet. He just needed time to find Snuffles and get him back in his cage. A search party – that was it. He hurried to the phone.

Soon after, Darren arrived. The two of them searched the house from top to bottom. But there was no sign of Snuffles. Not even a tiny trail of hamster poo.

"Boy, you are in big trouble!" said Darren, as they went out into the garden. "Miss Boot will go up the wall. She'll murder you!"

Darren's right, thought Bertie. Miss Boot

was fonder of Snuffles than she was of most of her class. Bertie had heard her talking to him in a soppy, baby voice.

"He must be somewhere. Keep looking!" he said.

"And what about us?" Darren went on. "He was our hamster too. I'm going to miss him!"

"Then help me find him!" said Bertie.

Whiffer was dozing under the garden bench. He yawned contentedly.

"Darren," said Bertie. "You don't think…?"

Darren looked at Whiffer. "Naaa! Don't be stupid! He wouldn't!"

"No," agreed Bertie. All the same, Whiffer would chase anything – squirrels especially. And to a dog, a fluffy hamster looked much like a squirrel. What if

Dirty Bertie

Whiffer had chased Snuffles? What if he had caught him and… Bertie couldn't bear to think about it. Everyone at school would blame him!

"What are we going to do?" he moaned.

Darren shrugged. "Don't ask me! You're the one who lost him!"

"But what if we can't find him?"

"You'll just have to face Miss Boot.
Or else buy another one."

Another hamster! thought Bertie. *That's
not such a bad idea.* He could look in
the pet shop for one like Snuffles. There
was just one problem.

"I don't have any money," he said.

They were silent for a while, lost in
thought. Suddenly Bertie leaped to his
feet.

"We could make one!" he cried.

"What?"

"A hamster –
out of fur 'n' stuff.
You know, like a
teddy bear."

Darren snorted.
"Miss Boot won't fall for that. It'll just sit
there like a blob."

"That won't matter!" said Bertie. "We'll just say he's asleep. Snuffles is always asleep!"

Darren considered it. "But what about him eating?"

"*We'll* feed him," said Bertie. "The two of us. We'll just pretend and stuff the food in our pockets."

"It'll never work," said Darren. "Miss Boot will find out."

"Not if we're careful. Anyway, it's only till I can save up for a new one."

Darren still looked doubtful. It sounded potty to him. Trying to pass off some stuffed bit of fur as Snuffles? But Bertie was convinced it would work – and besides, they didn't have a better idea.

CHAPTER 4

Monday morning arrived – the first day back at school. Class 3 trooped into their room under the stern eye of Miss Boot. Bertie tried to sneak past, carrying Snuffles' cage.

"BERTIE!" barked Miss Boot.

Uh oh. Bertie stopped in his tracks.

"I'll just, er, put Snuffles back," he said.

"Come here!" said Miss Boot. "I want to check that he's all right."

Bertie plodded over miserably.

"I hope you looked after him properly," said Miss Boot. "Did you feed him every day, and clean out his cage?"

"Yes, yes," said Bertie. "Can I put him back now?"

"Wait," said Miss Boot. "I haven't seen him yet."

Bertie's heart sank. This was just what he'd been dreading. The class crowded round, eager to get a glimpse of their favourite hamster. Bertie set down the cage.

"Where is he?" asked Miss Boot.

"There," said Bertie. "He's asleep."

All Miss Boot could see was a furry lump, hidden under piles of straw.

"He looks fatter," she frowned.

"No, I don't think so," said Bertie.

"What have you been feeding him?"

"Just the usual hamster stuff."

Miss Boot prodded the furry lump with her finger. "He's not moving!" she squawked.

Bertie gulped. He got ready to run.

Miss Boot gave Snuffles another prod. He slumped on his side.

"Ohhh!" The children gasped.

Miss Boot reached into the cage and brought Snuffles out. She stared at the rolled-up sock covered in sticky fur. It had a lopsided smile and two goggly eyes.

"BERTIE!" thundered Miss Boot. "WHAT DO YOU CALL THIS?"

Bertie turned very pale. "Crumbs," he said. "I've been looking for that sock."

Dirty Bertie

WHAM!

The front door slammed shut. Bertie drooped into the kitchen and threw his bag on the floor. Mum was sorting through a pile of wet washing.

"Good day at school?" she asked.

"Terrible," groaned Bertie, flopping into a chair.

"Did you take Snuffles back?" asked Mum.

"Oh, um, yeah, of course."

"Really? I expect Miss Boot was pleased to see him?"

"Yes, very pleased," said Bertie.

"That's funny," said Mum. "Because when I checked through your dirty washing basket I found something."

Dirty Bertie

She pointed to a cardboard box on the worktop.

Bertie went over. He looked inside.

"SNUFFLES!" he cried. "YOU'RE ALIVE!"

"No thanks to you," said Mum. "He could have ended up in the washing machine. Why didn't you tell me he'd got out?"

"I thought you might be cross," said Bertie.

He scooped up Snuffles and cuddled him. He never thought he'd be so pleased to see him.

"Clever boy," he grinned. "Wait till I tell Miss Boot."

Mum smiled. "Well, he certainly seems pleased to see you."

"How can you tell?" asked Bertie.

"Because he's just pooed on your jumper."

Dirty Bertie

CHAPTER 1

It was Saturday morning. Mum was tidying the kitchen. Bertie was still in his dressing gown, eating breakfast. "Listen," he said. "I can burp my name…"

He took a deep breath.

"*BURPIE!*"

Mum groaned. "Bertie! Please!"

"What? I bet you can't do it."

"I don't want to," said Mum. "It's disgusting!"

Bertie didn't see why. At school he was the champion burper of his class. He'd been practising for weeks. His longest burp was a record-breaking six seconds.

"Get dressed," said Mum. "Mrs Smugly's coming and she's bringing Flora."

Bertie groaned. "FLORA? What for?"

"Because I invited her mum for coffee."

"You don't even like her!" grumbled Bertie.

"Of course I do!"

"You don't!" said Bertie. "You told Dad she's stuck up and she never stops boasting about Flora."

Mum wiped the table. "Well, Flora is very talented. You should try to be more like her."

Dirty Bertie

"Huh! No thanks!" said Bertie, scornfully. Who wanted to be like goody-goody Flora? Last time she came he'd had to sit through hours of her playing the clarinet. The way her mum went on, you'd think she was some kind of genius. *Anyway,* thought Bertie, *I bet Flora can't burp for six seconds.*

DING DONG!

"They're here," groaned Mum. "For heaven's sake, Bertie, get dressed."

Bertie stomped up to his room. He got changed as slowly as he could. But then he remembered the chocolate biscuits that Mum always kept for visitors. He hurried downstairs.

Dirty Bertie

There were only three biscuits left
on the plate. Bertie helped himself as he
sat down.

"And how is Flora doing at school?"
asked Mum.

"Oh, wonderfully!" said Mrs Smugly.
"She came top in maths again, didn't you
darling?"

Flora nodded. She eyed Bertie and
took a biscuit, leaving only one.

"As for ballet, Miss Leotard says she's
quite outstanding," said Mrs
Smugly. "Does Bertie
go to ballet?"

Dirty Bertie

"Er, no, not really," said Mum.

Bertie scowled. Did he look like he went to ballet?

Mrs Smugly chattered on. "Of course, it's hard to fit it all in. Ballet on Saturdays, clarinet Mondays, French classes Tuesday. Does Bertie speak French?"

"Not yet," said Mum. "I'm sure he will."

"Perhaps when he's older," said Mrs Smugly. "Flora's lucky — she's just so gifted. What a pity we didn't bring her clarinet."

"Mmm. What a pity," yawned Mum.

Bertie reached for the last chocolate biscuit. It was gone! Who had swiped it? Flora smiled sweetly and stuck out a sticky tongue at him.

"And what about you, Bertie?" asked Mrs Smugly.

Dirty Bertie

"Mmm?" said Bertie.

"How's the trumpet?"

Bertie looked blank. *Trumpet? What trumpet?*

"You know, Bertie," said Mum, nodding at him. "Actually he's doing very well. He's taking Grade 5, aren't you, Bertie?"

Bertie stared. *Grade 5? Taking it where?*

Mrs Smugly raised her eyebrows. "Grade 5? That is impressive. I'd love to hear you play sometime, Bertie."

So would I, thought Bertie. His mum was avoiding his eye. There was definitely something funny going on.

CHAPTER 2

That evening over supper Bertie mentioned what had happened.

"She told them WHAT?" said Dad.

"That I play the trumpet," repeated Bertie. "It turns out I'm really good."

"YOU? Play the trumpet?" hooted Suzy.

Mum had gone rather red. "Um, anyone for more potato?" she asked.

"But you don't even play an instrument!" said Dad.

"I do! I play the recorder!"

"Once," said Dad. "Until you broke it." He looked at Mum. "But what on earth made you say he plays the trumpet?"

Mum turned redder still. She wished Bertie had kept quiet.

"I had to say something," she sighed. "I was sick of hearing about fabulous Flora. I just mentioned that Bertie likes music."

"LIKES MUSIC?" cried Bertie. "You told them I play the *trumpet*!"

"Well, you might. You must be good at something."

"I am!" said Bertie. "I can burp for six whole seconds!"

"In any case," said Dad, ignoring him. "You'll have to explain it's not true."

"I can't do that now," said Mum. "It will look as if I told a lie."

"You did!" laughed Suzy.

"Well yes, but only to Mrs Smugly, and she'll never find out."

BRINGG! BRINGG!

The phone rang. Mum hurried to answer it, glad to escape. But when she returned she looked rather pale.

"That was Barbara Smugly," she said. "She asked if Bertie could play in a concert, with the Pudsley Junior Orchestra."

"HA HA!" howled Suzy. "Imagine that!"

"I hope you said 'no'?" said Dad.

Mum bit her lip. "Not exactly. I sort of agreed."

PLUUUUUUGHHHHH!
A lump of mash flew from
Bertie's mouth.

"WHAT?" he gasped.

"I'm sorry," said Mum.
"I couldn't get out of it! She'd
already put your name down."

"A concert?" cried Bertie. "But I don't
play the trumpet! I haven't even got one!"

"We'll hire one from a shop," said
Mum, desperately. "It won't be so bad.
Just a few rehearsals."

Rehearsals! This was getting worse and
worse! Well, he wouldn't do it. After all,
none of this was his fault.

"You can't be serious," said Dad.
"They'll find out he can't play."

"They won't," said Mum. "It's an
orchestra. There'll be dozens of children.

Who's going to notice if Bertie isn't playing?"

"No one," answered Bertie. "Cos I'm not doing it."

"You have to!" pleaded Mum. "I've promised."

"No way!" said Bertie.

Mum sighed. She'd dug herself into a deep hole. If Bertie backed out now, Mrs Smugly would want to know why. And what if she found out the truth? No, Bertie would just have to go through with it, and there was one way to persuade him.

"Bertie, you know that restaurant you like?" said Mum.

Bertie gasped. "Pizza Pronto?" Pizza Pronto served the biggest, yummiest pizzas in the world.

"Yes. There's one opposite the concert hall."

"Can we go? Please!" begged Bertie.

"Okay," said Mum. "As long as you play in the concert."

Bertie hesitated. This was bribery. On the other hand it was the best pizza in the world.

"It's a deal," he said.

Dad groaned. Bertie playing the trumpet – in a concert? This could only end in disaster.

CHAPTER 3

Rehearsals took place every Tuesday
at Pudsley Hall. When Bertie arrived
for his first practice the other children
were seated on the stage. They clutched
violins, flutes, trombones and tubas. A girl
struggled with a cello twice her size.
Bertie looked round for somewhere to sit.
He spotted Flora practising her clarinet.

Dirty Bertie

"Hello," he said, sitting down.

"You can't sit there," said Flora, rudely.

"Why not?"

"*Duh!* You're with the trumpets. Over there with Nigel."

Bertie clambered over chairs and music stands to reach his place. There were two boys, both holding shiny trumpets. The one called Nigel wore a velvet bow tie.

"Hello, I'm Bertie," said Bertie, sitting down.

"You can't sit there," snapped Nigel.

"Why not?"

Dirty Bertie

"That's for first trumpets. Second trumpets sit behind."

Bertie sighed wearily. "Does it matter?"

"Of course it matters!" said Nigel. "I'm first trumpet because I'm better than you. Why do you think I'm playing the solo?"

Bertie rolled his eyes.

"Go on then! Move!" ordered Nigel.

Bertie moved to the seat behind.

The conductor, Mr Quaver, arrived. He droned on about the music they were going to play. Bertie yawned. He got his trumpet out. Surely it couldn't be that difficult to play? He took a deep breath.

Pffft! Pfffft!

Not a sound. He tried again, holding down the keys. Nothing.

Dirty Bertie

Then he noticed a small key he hadn't yet tried. Bertie pressed it. A glob of spit dripped on the floor.

Wow! thought Bertie. *A dribble key!*

Mr Quaver finished talking and asked them to open their music. Bertie stared at the page – it was covered with squiggly black tadpoles.

Mr Quaver tapped his stand. He raised his baton and the orchestra began to play. The violins scraped. The flutes tootled. The drums boomed. Nigel and the others raised their trumpets. Bertie copied.

PAA PA-PA PA PAAA!

Pfft! Pfft! went Bertie, not getting a note.

The trumpets rested. The music went on. Bertie noticed Nigel raise his trumpet, ready for his solo. Bertie leaned forward and pressed his dribble key.

"EWWWWW!" howled Nigel, leaping to his feet.

"What on earth's the matter?" asked the conductor.

"Something dribbled down my neck!" Nigel swung round, glaring at Bertie. Bertie smiled back.

"Nigel!" sighed Mr Quaver. "Can we please get on?"

Bertie sat back in his seat and smiled. Maybe rehearsals wouldn't be so bad after all.

Over the next weeks, Bertie's trumpet practice drove his family mad. At first he couldn't get a note but eventually he got the hang of it. Terrible noises came from his bedroom – parps and poops and

Dirty Bertie

deafening squeaks.
Dad said it
sounded like a
herd of trumping
elephants. Suzy
went about
with her fingers
in her ears. Mum
said she wished
she'd never given Bertie
the trumpet in the first place. One
evening she decided they needed to
have a talk.

"Bertie," she said, "it's nice you want
to practise, but I'm not asking you to
actually play in the concert."

Bertie shrugged. "It's okay. I want to."

"Yes, but it's better if you don't."

"Why?" asked Bertie.

"Because, well … you can't really play the trumpet!"

"I was playing just now!" said Bertie.

"Yes, but a concert is different," said Mum. "There's an audience. If you make that horrible noise people will hear!"

"I want them to hear," said Bertie.

"That's the whole point," said Mum. "They'll realize you can't play."

Bertie frowned. "So what you're saying is, I just have to sit there and pretend?"

"Yes," said Mum. "Pretend but don't play."

"Not even a bit?"

"No," said Mum firmly. "Remember, no playing or no Pizza Pronto."

Bertie sighed. There was no pleasing some people – they just didn't appreciate good music.

CHAPTER 4

The night of the big concert finally
arrived. Bertie fiddled nervously with his
clip-on bow tie. He'd never performed
in a concert before. He would be
playing (or not playing) in front of
hundreds of people, including his whole
family. Still, what could possibly go
wrong? All he had to do was pretend.

Dirty Bertie

It was a small price to pay for a Pizza
Pronto Cheese Feast pizza.

His family came with him to the
dressing room. Mrs
Smugly was there
brushing Flora's hair.

"Hello, Bertie," she trilled. "I'm so
looking forward to hearing you play!"

"Me too!" grinned Suzy.

Mum nudged her to keep quiet.

Dirty Bertie

Just then, Mr Quaver hurried in, looking flustered. "Disaster!" he cried. "Nigel's got a tummy bug! He can't come, and he's playing the solo!"

Mrs Smugly tutted. "Well, surely someone else can do it? What about Bertie?"

"M-ME?" gasped Bertie.

"Yes, your mum's always saying how talented you are. Here's your big chance!"

Mum gulped. "But surely—"

"Splendid! That's settled, then!" interrupted Mr Quaver.

"I'm sure you'll be marvellous!" said Mrs Smugly, patting Bertie on the head.

Bertie felt sick. This wasn't happening! He'd wanted to play his trumpet, but not by himself. How could he play a solo when he could barely manage two notes?

Dirty Bertie

The audience clapped as the Pudsley
Junior Orchestra walked onstage. Bertie
could see his family in the front row.
Gran waved. Suzy gave him a thumbs up.
Next to her, Mrs Smugly clapped madly.
Bertie glanced at the exits. Maybe if he
made a run for it now he could escape?
But Mr Quaver was marching onstage
and bowing to the audience. He raised

his baton. The concert began.

The violins swelled. The flutes tootled.
The drums boomed. Bertie pretended
to join in with the trumpets. He was
sweating. He should never have let his
mum talk him into this. On and on went
the music, rising and falling. Suddenly
he noticed it had gone very quiet. Mr
Quaver's baton was pointing at him.
Yikes! The trumpet solo! This was his big
moment.

Dirty Bertie

Bertie stood up and raised his trumpet to his lips. He blew.

Pffft! Pfffttt!

Nothing.

Pffft!

Silence.

He blew with all his might. A single note wailed out like a dying bluebottle.

PAAAARRRRRRRPPPP!

The audience gasped. Bertie's mum went bright red. Mrs Smugly looked as if she was going to pass out. Next to her, Gran and Suzy were shaking with laughter.

Bertie lowered his trumpet, bowed and sat down. All in all he felt it hadn't gone too badly. At least he'd still be going to Pizza Pronto.

Dirty Bertie

After the concert, Bertie's family collected him from the dressing room.

"Come on," hissed Mum. "Let's get out of here before anyone sees us!"

But at that moment, the door opened and in walked Mrs Smugly. She bore down on them like a battleship.

"Never!" she fumed. "Never in my life have I heard anything so dreadful! Your son ruined the whole evening!"

Gran grinned. "I quite enjoyed it."

Mrs Smugly ignored her and rounded on Bertie. "The truth. Have you taken any music exams?"

"Well, um ... no," admitted Bertie.

"And have you ever in your life had a trumpet lesson?"

Bertie shook his head.

"Just as I thought," snapped Mrs Smugly, glaring at Mum. "He can't speak French, he doesn't go to ballet and he can't play the trumpet. Tell me, is there anything he *can* do?"

"Actually there is," said Bertie. "Do you want to hear?"

He took a deep breath...

BURPIE

For Daniel Barrie ~ D R

For Liz and Stephen – Our Friends in
the North ~ A M

Contents

OUCH!

CHAPTER 1

"Go on," said Darren. "I dare you. Before he comes back."

Bertie looked at the hammer. It belonged to Mr Grouch, the demon caretaker. Bertie and Darren were helping him with the scenery for the school play. So far they had done nothing but stand around listening to the caretaker grumble.

But Mr Grouch wasn't around right now. He'd gone off to fetch more nails, leaving his hammer lying on the stage.

"Why don't you do it?" asked Bertie.

"I dared you first," said Darren.

"I dare you back," said Bertie.

"I double dare you no returns," said Darren.

Bertie looked around. He never refused a dare, not even the time Darren dared him to lock Mr Weakly in the store cupboard. And this was just one little tap with a hammer. What harm could it do? A nail was sticking up practically begging to be hit. Bertie picked up the hammer and took a swing.

"Watch what you're doing!" cried Darren, ducking out of the way.

Dirty Bertie

"Well, stand back then," said Bertie.
"I need room."

He glanced round, checking that no
one was about. All clear.

DINK! He tapped the nail on the head.

Darren rolled his eyes. "Not like that!
Give it a proper whack."

Dirty Bertie

Bertie held the nail between his finger and thumb. He swung the hammer back and brought it down.

THUNK!

"YOWWWWW!" he wailed, dropping the hammer.

"What did you do?" said Darren.

"I HIT MY THUMB! ARGH! OWW!" Bertie hopped around like a frog on a dance floor.

"SHHH!" hissed Darren. "Someone will hear you!"

Bertie was in too much pain to care. "OWW! OWW! OWW!" he howled.

Footsteps came thudding down the corridor. Mr Grouch burst into the hall, followed by Miss Boot.

Dirty Bertie

"WHAT IS GOING ON?" yelled Miss Boot.

"Nothing, Miss," said Darren.

"ARGH! OHHHH!" cried Bertie, doubled over in pain.

Mr Grouch spotted the hammer on the floor.

"Have you been playing with this?" he growled, picking it up.

Darren shook his head. "No," he said. "*I* haven't!"

Miss Boot turned on Bertie. "Did you touch this hammer?"

"I was only trying to help!" moaned Bertie.

"I knew it!" cried Mr Grouch. "I turn my back for two seconds and this is what happens. That boy is a menace. He should be expelled!"

Dirty Bertie

"Yes, thank you, Mr Grouch," said Miss Boot. "I will deal with this."

"OWW! OWW!" wailed Bertie. "I think it's broken!"

"Don't make such a fuss!" snapped Miss Boot. "Let me see."

Dirty Bertie

Bertie let go of his thumb and held it out for inspection. Yikes! It had turned purple and swollen up like a balloon! "I don't feel very well," he said, going pale.

Miss Boot took charge. "Darren, take him to Miss Skinner's office," she ordered. "And Bertie, don't think you've heard the last of this, I shall be speaking to your parents."

Bertie sat outside Miss Skinner's office nursing his injured thumb. It was wrapped in a wet paper towel. He couldn't believe the way everyone was remaining so calm. Why hadn't they called an ambulance? For all they knew he could be dying!

The door flew open and his mum hurried in.

"Bertie, are you all right?" she cried.

Bertie shook his head weakly and held up his hand.

"I think it's broken!" he moaned.

"Your hand?"

"My thumb."

"Well, what happened?"

"It wasn't my fault," said Bertie. "I was trying to help. The hammer slipped."

"Hammer!" shrieked Mum. "What on earth were you doing with a hammer?"

"Hammering," replied Bertie.

"Well next time, *don't*. Hammers are dangerous," said Mum. "Let me see."

Bertie gingerly unwrapped the soggy paper towel. His thumb was still swollen.

Mum stared. "Is that it?" she said. "I thought it was serious!"

"It hurts!" said Bertie. "It's probably broken!"

"So you keep saying," sighed Mum. "Well, we'd better get it checked out. Let's get you to hospital."

CHAPTER 2

Later that afternoon, Bertie sat in the hospital waiting room. It was packed with people. Bertie stared at a small girl with her foot in plaster. Beside her was a man in a neck collar and a boy with a saucepan jammed on his head. You got all kinds of people in hospitals. Bertie checked his thumb again to see

Dirty Bertie

if it had got any bigger. It hadn't.

He looked at the clock. They had been waiting for hours and he hadn't eaten since lunch. His stomach gurgled. If they waited much longer he might pass out with hunger. Tempting smells drifted across from the snack bar.

"Mum, can I get some crisps?" asked Bertie.

"No," said Mum. "I thought you were in agony."

"I AM," said Bertie. "But crisps might take my mind off it."

Mum gave him a weary look. "You're not having crisps now," she said.

Bertie sighed. "How about a doughnut, then?"

"NO, BERTIE!" snapped Mum. "Just sit quietly and wait for the doctor."

Dirty Bertie

Bertie slumped in his seat. Talking about food only made him hungrier. Maybe he could just investigate what the snack bar had to offer? He got up.

"Where are you going?" asked Mum, lowering her magazine.

"Nowhere! Just to have a look," pleaded Bertie.

"Well, stay where I can keep an eye on you," said Mum.

There was a queue of people at the counter. Bertie hung around for a while, hoping someone might take pity on a starving boy. No one did. On a nearby table he noticed a bowl containing small packets of mayonnaise, tomato ketchup and mustard. Bertie slipped a couple of them into his pocket as emergency supplies for later. He looked up and

Dirty Bertie

found a boy with his arm in a sling watching him.

"What happened to you?" asked Bertie.

The boy shrugged. "Hit a lamp post."

"With your arm?" said Bertie.

"No, on my bike," said the boy.

"I hit my thumb with a hammer," said Bertie, proudly. He unwound the paper towel to show off his swollen thumb.

The boy shrugged. "Huh! That's nothing," he scoffed. "I'm always in hospital. This is the second time I broke my arm. Broke my collar bone too."

"Wow!" said Bertie, impressed. The only thing he'd ever broken was the upstairs toilet.

The boy lowered his voice. "They don't let you stay unless it's serious," he said.

"Stay where?" said Bertie.

"On the children's ward." The boy gave him a pitying look. "Haven't you ever been in hospital?"

Bertie shook his head.

"You don't know what you're missing!" said the boy. "You don't have to do nothing – just lie in bed all day, watching TV. No going to school – nothing."

Bertie gawped at the boy. Staying in

hospital sounded like paradise! Much better than listening to Miss Boot droning on for hours. Maybe the hospital would keep him in for a few days, or even a week? He noticed his mum beckoning him to sit down.

"Better go," he said.

The boy nodded. "Okay. Maybe catch you on the children's ward later?"

"I'll be there," said Bertie.

He went back to his seat.

"Who was that?" asked Mum.

"Don't know," replied Bertie. "We just got talking. Mum, how long do you think I'll have to stay in hospital?"

Mum laughed. "Bertie, you've only bruised your thumb!"

"It might be broken," Bertie reminded her.

Mum shook her head. "If it was, you'd be in agony."

"I *am* in agony!" said Bertie. "I'm just not making a fuss!"

"You fooled me," said Mum. "In any case, they'll probably just give you a plaster and send you home."

Bertie stared. Send him home with a plaster? They couldn't do that! What about missing school?

CHAPTER 3

"BERTIE BURNS?" called a loud voice. Bertie looked up. A red-haired nurse with a clipboard was looking round the waiting room. Her badge said "Nurse Nettles".

"Over here!" said Mum, standing up.

"Follow me, would you please?" said the nurse.

Dirty Bertie

Bertie and Mum followed her down the corridor and into a cubicle with a bed, a table and a couple of plastic chairs. The nurse drew the curtain across and looked briskly at Bertie.

"Well, young man, what have you been up to?" she said.

"Nothing," frowned Bertie. "I hurt my thumb."

"He hit it with a hammer," explained Mum.

"Not on purpose," said Bertie. The way everyone talked you'd think he had.

Nurse Nettles wrote something on a form. "Let's have a look at it then, shall we?" she said.

Bertie winced as Nurse Nettles unwound the paper towel. The thumb was still purple, though not quite as

Dirty Bertie

swollen as Bertie remembered.

"Mmm, yes, I see," said Nurse Nettles.
"Try and move it for me."

Bertie waggled his thumb gingerly.

"OUCH!" he yelled.

"Now bend it back."

Bertie bent it back.

"ARGHH!"

"Well?" asked Mum. "Is it serious?"

Nurse Nettles smiled. "I don't think
so. Badly bruised, that's all."

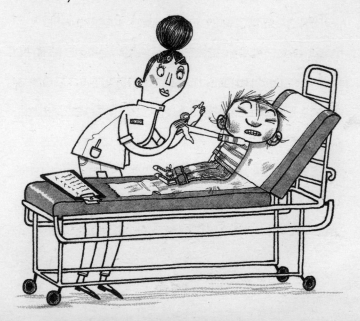

"BRUISED?" cried Bertie. "Not broken?"

"Not broken," said Nurse Nettles. "But we'll get Dr Dose to examine you."

This was more like it.

"Does that mean I have to stay in hospital?" asked Bertie.

Nurse Nettles laughed. "No, don't worry, you'll be going home in no time."

She went off to find the doctor.

Bertie slumped back on the bed. Bruised? Was that all? It was so unfair! After all the pain he'd been through! Had Nurse Nettles actually looked at his thumb properly? It was purple! Did they really expect him to go to school with a purple thumb? What he needed was a proper rest – rest and unlimited television.

"You see?" said Mum. "I told you it was nothing to worry about."

Dirty Bertie

Bertie scowled. If only his thumb was hanging off, spurting fountains of blood everywhere. If only it had gone bad and was dripping with yellow pus. Wait a moment… Bertie felt in his pocket. He still had the little packets he'd got from the snack bar. Mustard was yellow. All he needed was a minute to himself, before the doctor came.

He jumped to his feet. "I need the toilet!" he said.

"What? Now?" said Mum. "Can't you wait?"

"No!" said Bertie. "Won't be a minute." He dashed off.

CHAPTER 4

By the time Bertie got back, Dr Dose had arrived and was talking to his mum and Nurse Nettles.

"Right then," said Dr Dose, rubbing his hands. "Let's have a look at this thumb, shall we?"

Bertie nodded weakly and held it up for him to see.

Dirty Bertie

"Good heavens!" said Nurse Nettles.

Bertie's thumb had turned a funny colour. Globs of yellow oozed and dripped on to the floor.

"What happened?" cried Mum.

"I don't know!" groaned Bertie. "I think it's infected!"

Dr Dose pushed his glasses up his nose. "It does look odd. Let me see."

He peered closely at the thumb. "Cotton wool, please, nurse," he said.

He dabbed at the messy thumb and sniffed the cotton wool.

"Ah," he said. "Just as I thought. Mustarditis."

Nurse Nettles giggled.

Bertie looked up at them. "Is that bad?"

"Very bad," said Doctor Dose.

"Mustarditis?" repeated Mum.

Dr Dose gave her a wink. "Perhaps you could wait outside while I talk to Bertie."

"Yes, I think *someone* should," said Mum.

Bertie sat on the bed. His brilliant trick had fooled everyone. *Children's ward, here I come!* he thought. *A whole week off school!*

"Will I have to stay in hospital?" he asked, feebly.

"For a while," said Dr Dose. "After the operation."

Dirty Bertie

Bertie gasped. Operation? No one had said anything about an operation!

"W-what?" he mumbled.

"Well, your thumb's turned yellow," said Dr Dose. "Very bad, mustarditis. The only thing is to operate right away. Wouldn't you agree, Nurse Nettles?"

Nurse Nettles nodded, trying not to laugh.

Bertie stared at them. All he wanted was a few days off school – not this! He imagined the operating theatre. There would be an injection – with a long needle. Doctors in masks. What if they decided his thumb couldn't be saved? What if they chopped it off? He needed his thumb to beat Darren at Mega Monster Racing!

Dirty Bertie

Dr Dose put something on. It was a green mask.

"Right," he said brightly. "Shall we get started?"

"NOOO!" cried Bertie, leaping off the bed.

He rushed through the curtains, hurrying past his mum, who was waiting outside.

Dirty Bertie

"HELP! SAVE ME!" he gasped. "Don't let them get me!"

"I thought your thumb was agony," said Mum.

"No!" said Bertie. "Look, it's better!" He licked his thumb. "It was only mustard."

Dr Dose and Nurse Nettles peered through the curtains. They were laughing and wiping their eyes. Bertie gaped. The truth dawned on him. There was no operation – it was all a joke.

"So," said Mum. "Mustard, eh?"

"Um, yes," said Bertie. "I must have somehow got a bit on my thumb."

"Really? I wonder how that could have happened," said Mum dryly.

"Never mind," said Nurse Nettles brightly. "Let's find you a plaster, shall we?"

Dirty Bertie

Bertie went back to sit on the bed.
A plaster – after all he'd been through!
He'd told Darren his thumb was broken
and by now the story would be all
round school. No one was going to be
very impressed if he came back wearing
a stupid little plaster.

Nurse Nettles looked in a drawer.
She held out a plaster the size of a
postage stamp. Bertie looked at her.

"Actually," he said, "you don't have
something a bit bigger, do you?"

Dirty Bertie

CHAPTER 1

"LAST ONE CHANGED IS A STINKER!" shouted Darren.

Bertie banged into the cubicle and dumped his bag on the seat. It was Friday – swimming day. He stripped off his clothes, dropping them in a messy heap. Then he picked up his bag and emptied it out. Goggles, towel, shower gel…

Wait a minute, where were his swimming trunks? His heart missed a beat.

He picked up his towel and shook it out. Nothing! He searched the bottom of his bag. Empty! Surely he hadn't … he couldn't have left his swimming trunks at home? Miss Boot would go up the wall!

He wrapped a towel round his waist and climbed on to the seat.

"Psssst! Eugene!" he hissed, peering into the next cubicle.

"What?" Eugene blinked at him through his goggles.

"I forgot my trunks!" said Bertie.

"You're joking!" said Eugene.

Darren's head popped up from the next cubicle along. "What's going on?"

"Bertie's forgotten his trunks," explained Eugene.

Dirty Bertie

"You haven't!"

"I HAVE!" groaned Bertie. "You've got to help! Miss Boot will kill me!"

His friends nodded grimly. A few weeks ago Trevor had forgotten his towel. Miss Boot had made him do twenty laps of the changing room to dry off.

"What am I going to do?" moaned Bertie.

Darren shrugged. "You'll just have to wear your pants."

Bertie gave him a look. "I can't swim in my pants!" he said. His pants had holes in them and, besides, they looked like … well, like pants. He turned to Eugene.

"Didn't you bring a spare pair?"

"Why would I do that?" asked Eugene.

"So I can borrow them, of course!"

Eugene shook his head.

"Darren, what about you?" pleaded Bertie.

"Sorry, can't help," said Darren.

Bertie gave a heavy sigh. He was sunk.

There was a loud bang on the changing-room door.

"ONE MINUTE! GET A MOVE ON!" bellowed Miss Boot.

"Sorry, Bertie, we better go," said Eugene. "You know how mad she gets if you're late."

Dirty Bertie

"Yeah," said Darren. "Good luck!"

The two of them hurried out, leaving Bertie alone. He slumped on the seat in despair. Suddenly, an ugly face appeared in the gap under the door. It was Know-All Nick, the last person on earth he wanted to see.

Dirty Bertie

"Oh dear, Bertie, forgotten your swimming trunks?" he jeered. "Wait till Miss Boot finds out!" He disappeared, sniggering to himself.

Bertie sank back against the wall. Maybe if he just stayed here, he wouldn't be missed and the swimming lesson would go ahead without him. Afterwards he could wet his hair under the tap and slip on to the coach.

WHAM! The changing-room door flew open. Footsteps thudded down the corridor.

"BERTIE! WHERE ARE YOU?" boomed Miss Boot. "Come out of there!"

"I can't!" moaned Bertie. "I haven't got any trunks!"

Miss Boot raised her eyes to heaven. Why did it always have to be Bertie?

"Open this door!" she ordered.

Bertie slid back the lock and peeped
out, holding the towel round his waist.

"Couldn't I just sit and watch?" he
pleaded.

"Certainly not!" snapped Miss Boot.
"You'll just have to borrow some trunks."

"I've tried!" said Bertie. "No one's got any."

"Then go to Reception and ask them to lend you a pair," said Miss Boot. "And get a move on. Everyone's waiting!"

Bertie nodded and shuffled past Miss Boot. As he reached the door, he trod on his towel.

"Bertie!" Miss Boot groaned and covered her eyes.

CHAPTER 2

Bertie stood in Reception. The woman behind the desk was talking on the phone.

"Yes? Can I help you?" she said, putting it down at last.

"Um ... yes," said Bertie, "I don't have any swimming trunks."

"Oh dear!" said the woman. "Didn't you bring them?"

"I forgot," said Bertie. "They're probably at home – in my pants drawer."

"Well, you're not allowed in the pool without a costume, it's against the rules," said the woman.

"I know," said Bertie. "But Miss Boot said you might have some swimming trunks I could borrow."

"I see," sighed the woman. She looked at her coffee, which was getting cold. "Wait there," she said. "I'll see what I can do."

Bertie waited. It was embarrassing standing in the middle of Reception, wearing only a towel. A small girl over by the drinks machine was staring at him. Finally, the woman came back carrying a large green box, marked "Lost Property". She put it down on the floor.

Dirty Bertie

"Here we are," she said. "There's not much, but take your pick."

Bertie peered inside. The box contained a pair of orange water wings, a swimming cap, a spotty bikini and a single pair of swimming trunks. Bertie fished them out. They were silver Speedos, hardly bigger than a paper tissue.

"Is this all there is?" he gasped.

The woman sniffed. "Looks like it."

"But haven't you got anything else? Like normal swimming shorts?"

The woman glared. "We're not a shop!" she snapped. "Do you want them or not?"

Bertie nodded miserably. He had no choice. He shuffled back to the changing room, holding the trunks as if they were riddled with fleas. Wait till his friends saw him! He was going to be the laughing stock of the whole class.

He locked himself inside the cubicle and pulled on the silver trunks. They were so old that the elastic had gone, and no matter how tightly he tied them, they wouldn't stay up! He looked down in horror. There was no way he could wear these.

Dirty Bertie

Someone thumped on the door.
"BERTIE! HURRY UP!" thundered Miss
Boot. "WE'RE WAITING FOR YOU!"

Bertie groaned. He opened the
cubicle door and slunk out.

Miss Boot stared. "What on earth are
those?" she said.

"Swimming trunks," wailed Bertie. "It's
all they had!"

Dirty Bertie

"Very well, they'll have to do," said Miss Boot. "Pull them up and let's go."

The class were sitting by the side of the pool, with their feet in the water. Miss Crawl leaned against the rail, impatient to get started. She was a tall, thin woman who had once been Junior Backstroke Champion.

Everyone looked round as Bertie appeared. He ducked behind Miss Boot, but it was too late. Know-All Nick had seen him.

"HA HA! LOOK AT BERTIE!" he hooted.

"Nice trunks, Bertie!" giggled Donna.

"Are they your grandad's?" screeched Trevor.

Bertie glared at them and plodded over to join the end of the line.

Dirty Bertie

"Oh, Bertie," sang Nick. "We can see your bottom!"

Bertie went bright red and hitched up the saggy Speedos. This was terrible! How was he going to get through an entire swimming lesson without dying of embarrassment?

CHAPTER 3

Bertie clung to the side of the pool,
shivering with cold. The lesson had only
been going half an hour, but it felt like a
lifetime. He had hardly dared leave the
side for fear of losing his trunks.

Know-All Nick zoomed past, splashing
him in the face.

"BERTIE!" bellowed a voice.

Uh oh, Miss Boot had spotted him.

"What are you doing?" she called. "Miss Crawl, why isn't Bertie joining in?"

"Good question," said Miss Crawl. "Bertie, what do you think you're doing?"

"Nothing," said Bertie.

"Well, get away from the side. I said four lengths' breaststroke!"

"I can't!" wailed Bertie.

"Why not?"

"My trunks keep falling down!"

"No feeble excuses!" snapped Miss Crawl. "Get swimming!"

Bertie groaned. He pushed off and swam after the rest of the class. ARGHH! The saggy Speedos were falling down again! He could feel them slipping towards his knees. He tried swimming with one hand while holding on to the stupid trunks with the other. It was hard work. He kept sinking and glugging great gulps of water.

"Come on, Bertie, keep up!" shouted Darren, speeding past.

At last he made it to the far end and hung on to the rail, gasping for breath. Know-All Nick climbed out by the steps.

He hurried over to Miss Crawl,
dripping wet.

"Miss! OOOH! OOH! I need the
toilet!" he whimpered.

Miss Crawl scowled. "Can't you hang
on?"

"No! I've got to goooo!" cried Nick,
jiggling from foot to foot.

"Oh, very well!" sighed Miss Crawl. "Hurry up!"

Bertie watched Nick patter off towards the changing room. Suddenly, he was struck by an idea. It was so simple it was genius. But he'd have to move fast or it would be too late. Bertie swam to the steps and climbed out.

"What now?" said Miss Crawl.

"Miss! I need the toilet, Miss!" pleaded Bertie.

"Not you as well? You'll just have to wait till the lesson is over."

"But I can't!" said Bertie, dancing up and down. "I have to go! NOW!"

Miss Crawl sighed heavily. "Go on then. Make it quick!"

Dirty Bertie

Bertie pushed open the changing-room door. There was no one about. He stole over to the boys' toilets. He could hear Know-All Nick humming to himself in one of the cubicles. Bertie tiptoed over.
He got down on his hands and knees to peer under the door. There were Nick's two white feet dangling in mid-air, with his red swimming trunks round his ankles.

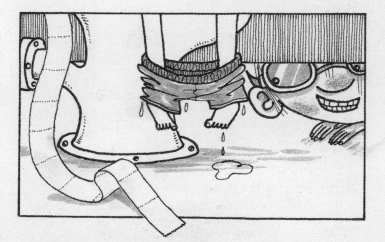

"Hmm hmm hmm!" Nick hummed to himself.

Slowly, silently, Bertie reached his hand under the door.

SNATCH!

He grabbed the red swimming trunks and yanked them off.

"ARGHHH!" cried Nick, overbalancing and falling off the toilet.

"HEY! GIVE THEM BACK!" he howled. "THEY'RE MINE!"

"Sorry, Nickerless!" replied Bertie. "I need them."

Nick banged on the door. "I'll tell!" he yelled. "You give them back, Bertie, or I'll tell!"

There was no reply.

Cautiously, Know-All Nick unlocked the door and came out. Bertie had vanished. All that remained was a soggy pair of Speedos lying on the floor.

CHAPTER 4

Back in the pool, Bertie joined the rest of the class.

PEEP! Miss Crawl blew her whistle. "Everyone out! Line up by the side!"

Eugene climbed out after Bertie. "Where did you get those trunks?" he asked, in surprise. "I thought yours were teeny-weeny."

Bertie grinned. "I'll tell you later."

"Right," said Miss Crawl. "I want you all to try the standing dive we did last week."

"Just a minute!" Miss Boot had been counting heads. "We're missing someone," she said. "Where is Nicholas?"

Miss Crawl frowned. "He went to the toilet, but that was ages ago."

Miss Boot marched over to the boys' changing room. She pounded on the door. THUMP! THUMP!

"Nicholas? Are you in there?"

No answer.

"NICHOLAS! Come out!"

"I CAN'T!" wailed a voice.

"Nonsense! What's the matter with you?" barked Miss Boot.

"I haven't got any trunks!"

"Don't be ridiculous, you were

wearing them earlier. Come out this
instant!"

"Please don't make me!" snivelled
Nick.

But Miss Boot was not a patient
woman. "If you're not out in ten seconds
I shall come in and drag you out," she
warned.

The door opened slowly and Know-
All Nick shuffled out. He was covering

himself with a small yellow towel.

"Line up then!" ordered Miss Boot.

"But Miss, Bertie's—"

"Line up, I said! You're keeping everyone waiting!"

Know-All Nick gulped. He drooped over to join the line and put down his towel. He was wearing the saggy silver Speedos.

"HA HA!" hooted Bertie.

"Hee hee! Nice trunks, Nick!" giggled Darren.

"QUIET!" bawled Miss Crawl. "On my whistle, you will all dive in. Arms out, knees bent, heads down."

PEEP!

SPLASH! SPLOOSH! The class flopped into the pool one by one. Bertie bobbed to the surface and wiped his eyes. Something was floating on top of the water. A pair of silver swimming trunks. Bertie fished them out and waved them in the air.

"OH, NICKERLESS!" he cried. "DID YOU LOSE SOMETHING?"

Dirty Bertie

BRAINIAC!

SWOTTER
18

PUDSLEY
01

CHAPTER 1

It was Tuesday morning. Miss Boot put away the register and took out a letter.

"I have some good news for you," she said. "In two weeks' time it's the Junior Quiz Challenge and we will be entering a team."

The class turned pale. Bertie groaned. Of all the horrible tortures teachers

had invented, the worst was the Junior
Quiz Challenge. Four children forced on
to a stage and made to answer endless
impossible questions: What is the capital
of Belgium? How many minutes in a
fortnight? Can you spell "ignoramus"?

Every year Pudsley Junior entered a
quiz team and every year they came
bottom. Last time they'd scored a grand
total of two and a half points – a record
low in the history of the competition.
A picture of the team had appeared
in the *Pudsley Post* under the headline:
"QUIZ FLOPS COME BOTTOM OF
THE CLASS!"
Miss Boot had been furious. Miss Skinner
said they'd brought shame on the
whole school.

Bertie slid down in his chair. There was

no way he wanted to be on the team.
He'd rather dance down the high street
dressed as a fairy. But wait a second, why
did he need to worry? Miss Boot never
picked him for anything.

"Hands up," said Miss Boot, "who'd
like to be on the quiz team?"

Only one hand went up. It belonged
to Know-All Nick. *Trust smarty-pants
Nick to volunteer*, thought Bertie.

"Nicholas!" beamed Miss Boot.
"Marvellous! I knew you
would set an example."

Nick's head swelled
even larger than usual.

Dirty Bertie

"Who else? What about you, Donna?"
asked Miss Boot.

"Umm…" said Donna.

"Excellent!" said Miss Boot. "And
Eugene, I'm sure you'd be good!"

"Er … ah … mmm," mumbled Eugene.

"Splendid! That's three then," said
Miss Boot. "So we just need one more
to complete the team." Her gaze swept
over the rows of faces. The class shrank
back, desperate to avoid her eye. Darren
raised his hand.

"What about Bertie, Miss?" he asked.

Bertie spun round. "Me? Are you
mad?" He glared at Darren. Then he
remembered. Yesterday he had put
superglue on Darren's chair and Darren
had vowed to get his revenge.

Miss Boot frowned. "I don't think so,"

Dirty Bertie

she said. "We need bright, clever children
and Bertie is … well, his talents lie in
other areas." This was true, thought Bertie.
He was the class burping champion and
he did a brilliant impression of Miss Boot.

"But, Miss, Bertie is brilliant at quizzes,"
claimed Darren, grinning at Bertie.

"NO I'M NOT!" cried Bertie.

"You are!" lied Darren. "You've always
got your head in a quiz book."

"Thank you, Darren, I'll bear that in mind," said Miss Boot. She turned back to the class. "One more volunteer," she said. "Who'd like to represent our school? Royston?"

Royston shook his head.

"Nisha?"

Nisha hid behind Donna.

"Kylie?"

Kylie looked as if she might be sick.

Dirty Bertie

Miss Boot sighed heavily. "Very well then, Bertie, you're on the team."

"But, Miss…!" moaned Bertie.

"No need to thank me," said Miss Boot. "Just remember, I am giving you a chance, Bertie. Last year's team did not make their school proud. But this year will be different, because you will be prepared. And when the time comes, I expect you to win – is that clear?"

The quiz team nodded their heads gloomily. Bertie glared at Darren. This was so unfair!

CHAPTER 2

DRRRRRING! The bell went for lunchtime. Bertie headed for the door.

"Bertie!" called Know-All Nick. "Quiz team meeting!"

Bertie rolled his eyes and flopped into a chair beside Eugene. Who wanted to be stuck inside listening to Nick, when you could be outside playing?

Dirty Bertie

"Now," said Nick, "Miss Boot told me to choose a team captain. I think we all know who it should be."

"Who?" said Donna.

"Well, me, obviously," said Nick.

"Why you?"

"Because I'm the cleverest," boasted Nick.

"The ugliest, you mean," muttered Bertie.

Nick ignored him. "Practice sessions will be *every* lunchtime, starting today."

"Every lunchtime?" groaned Eugene. "How can we practise for a quiz?"

"By answering test questions, of course," said Nick. "Miss Boot lent me this." He reached into his bag and brought out *The Bumper Book of Quiz Fun*.

"Right, I'll be quiz master," he said.

"And who's testing you?" asked Donna.

"No one, because I'm captain and I've got the book," said Nick. "Anyway, I don't need the practice. Bertie, you can go first because you're the most stupid. Eugene, you time him. You've got one minute."

Eugene set the timer on his watch.

"Donna, you keep the score. Ready?" said Nick, settling on a page in the book. "Go…! Hades was the god of what?"

"Never heard of him," said Bertie.

"He's a Greek god, stupid, like Zeus and Mars."

"Isn't that a chocolate bar?" said Bertie.

"What?"

"Mars."

"Yes! No! I'm asking the questions!" snapped Nick, getting muddled.

"Well, what's the good of asking me stuff I don't know?" grumbled Bertie. "Why don't you try asking me something I do know?"

Nick sighed. "Next question…"

"Time's up!" shouted Eugene.

"And in that round, Bertie, you answered no questions and scored no points!" said Donna.

Bertie took a bow. Eugene clapped.

"Yes, very funny," glowered Nick. "A fat lot of use you're going to be."

Dirty Bertie

After school, Bertie dropped in to see his gran. He told her all about the Junior Quiz Challenge and Miss Boot picking him for the team.

"That's wonderful, Bertie!" said Gran.

"No, it's terrible," said Bertie. "I'm rubbish at quizzes and Miss Boot expects us to win."

"Well, maybe you will," said Gran.

"We won't!" Bertie moaned. "We come last every year!"

Gran sighed. "Tell you what," she said, "why don't we call in at the library and find some books to help you."

Bertie couldn't see how books were going to help, but he didn't have any better ideas.

Dirty Bertie

At the library Gran took him upstairs to the Children's Section.

"So what kind of things do you like?" she asked.

Bertie shrugged. "Loads of things," he said. "Worms, slugs, maggots, stink-bombs…"

"Hmm," said Gran. "Somehow I doubt stink-bombs are going to help."

Dirty Bertie

Bertie looked along the shelves —
there was no way he could read this
many books. He might as well face it —
the quiz was going to be one big
disaster. They would end up losing by
a zillion points and Miss Boot would
blame him as usual. He trawled through
the books gloomily. *Ancient Kings and
Queens*, *Fun with Fossils*, *My First Book of
Flowers*... Wait a minute, what was this?

"Gran!" called Bertie. "Can I get this
one out?"

"Of course!"
said Gran.
"What is it?"

Bertie held
up the cover
so she could
read it.

CHAPTER 3

For the next two weeks, the quiz team
met to practise every lunchtime. Things
did not improve. Nick grumbled that he
was leading a team of idiots, even though
Donna and Eugene were quite good.
Sadly the same could not be said of
Bertie. The one time he got an answer
right, he ran round the room yelling with

his T-shirt over his head.

All too soon, the day of the Junior Quiz Challenge arrived. Pudsley had been drawn to face last year's finalists, Swotter House. As the coach pulled into the drive, Bertie stared up at the ancient-looking school. Miss Topping, one of the teachers, was waiting to meet them at the door.

"Miss Boot, welcome!" she beamed. "And this must be your quiz team!"

"Yes," said Miss Boot. "This is Nicholas, Donna, Eugene and … don't do that please, Bertie."

Bertie removed a finger that had crept up his nose. He wiped it on his jumper to show he hadn't forgotten his manners.

"Well," said Miss Topping brightly,

Dirty Bertie

"I'm sure they're cleverer than they look. May I introduce our team? This is Giles, Miles, Tara and Harriet. They are so looking forward to beating … I mean meeting you."

The Swotter House team shook hands solemnly. They wore spotless purple blazers and neatly knotted ties. Bertie thought they looked like they all belonged to the same family – the Frankenstein family.

Dirty Bertie

At two o'clock people began to file into the hall for the start of the quiz. The two teams were seated opposite each other on the stage. The Swotter House team sat up straight. The Pudsley team fidgeted nervously. Miss Boot was in the front row next to Miss Skinner. The hall was filling up with supporters from both schools. Bertie wondered if he should make a run for it now. Know-All Nick leaned over to give his team talk.

"Remember," he whispered. "I'm captain, so let me handle the questions."

"Yeah, but what if you don't know the answers?" said Bertie.

Nick rolled his eyes. "Trust me, I know what I'm doing," he said.

Dirty Bertie

Donna and Eugene exchanged
worried looks. But it was too late to
argue now, Miss Topping was taking her
seat and the quiz was about to start. The
hall lights dimmed. The audience chatter
died down. Miss Topping began by
explaining the rules.

Dirty Bertie

"The first team to buzz may answer," she said. "If you get it wrong, the question passes to the other team."

Both teams nodded. The Junior Quiz Challenge began.

"What do the letters MP stand for?" said Miss Topping.

PUDSLEY

BUZZ!

"More pudding!" shouted Nick.

"No, I'll pass it over," said Miss Topping.

"Member of Parliament," answered Giles.

"Correct! Who invented the telephone?"

BUZZ! Nick was first again.

"Um…" he said, going red. "Er … it was…"

"Time's up," said Miss Topping. "Swotter House?"

"Alexander Graham Bell," answered Giles.

"Correct!"

SWOTTER   18

PUDSLEY   0 1

CHAPTER 4

The questions went on – and on.
By round three Pudsley were trailing
miserably by 18 points to one. Nick had
answered 19 questions, and got 18 of
them wrong.

"What are you doing?" moaned
Donna, when they stopped for a
drinks break.

"We have to buzz first or we'll lose!" said Nick.

"We *are* losing," said Bertie.

"What's the good of buzzing first if you don't know the answer?" complained Eugene.

"It's not my fault!" grumbled Nick. "The questions are too hard!"

"Well, if you carry on like this they're going to batter us," said Bertie.

"Yes, and so will Miss Boot," said Eugene.

They glanced over at their class teacher whose face was like thunder.

"Let me or Eugene answer for a change," said Donna.

"What about me?" asked Bertie.

"Er, well, you too," said Donna. "But only if you're sure you know the answer."

Dirty Bertie

Round four got under way. It was about books.

"Who wrote *The BFG*?"

BUZZ!

Donna got there first.

"Roald Dahl," she answered.

"Correct!"

"Can you name the Famous Five?"

BUZZ!

The scoreboard ticked over. Three rounds later, Swotter House were not looking quite so smug. Thanks to Donna and Eugene, Pudsley had closed the gap to just three points at 34 points to 31. Bertie had still not spoken a word, except to ask if he could go to the toilet. Now everything depended on the final round. The teams leaned forward.

Dirty Bertie

"Our final round is about the human body," said Miss Topping.

Bertie suddenly sat up, paying attention. This was more like it. He'd been reading *Why are Bogeys Green?*, which had a lot to say about the human body.

"What is saliva?" asked Miss Topping.

BUZZ!

"A disease?" asked Giles.

"No, I'm afraid not."

"I know!" shouted Bertie. He buzzed. "Spit!"

"Correct," said Miss Topping. "Which part of the body has half a million sweat glands?"

BUZZ!

"YOUR FEET!" yelled Bertie.

"Correct. What do you produce more of when you're scared?"

Dirty Bertie

BUZZ!

"EARWAX!" cried Bertie.

His teammates stared at him. Surely this had to be wrong?

"Correct!" said Miss Topping. "What—"

BEEP! BEEP! BEEP! The timer interrupted, bringing the quiz to an end. The scores were level at 34 points each. Miss Topping announced the contest would be decided by a tiebreak question.

"Whoever answers correctly is the winner," she said, glaring at the Swotter House team.

The teams sat on the edge of their seats, their fingers poised to buzz. Miss Boot chewed her fingernails.

Dirty Bertie

"What did the Romans use as toothpaste?" asked Miss Topping.

The hall fell deadly silent. Seven faces looked blank. Bertie shut his eyes, trying to remember. Toothpaste, what did the Romans use as toothpaste – hadn't he read this somewhere? It was something to do with squirrels or hamsters or…

BUZZ!

"Was it yoghurt?" asked Harriet.

"No. Pudsley, can you answer?"

Everyone turned to Bertie. He opened his eyes.

"MOUSE BRAINS!" he cried.

"EWWW!" groaned the audience. Miss Boot sunk her head in her hands. Trust Bertie to ruin everything.

Dirty Bertie

Miss Topping sighed deeply. "Correct," she said. "Pudsley are the winners."

A deafening cheer shook the hall. Know-All Nick was speechless. Miss Boot and Miss Skinner hugged and danced round the room. For the first time ever, Pudsley had won a quiz contest, and Bertie, of all people, had answered the winning question. He ran round the stage yelling, until he was carried off by his cheering teammates.

"Well, we did it," said Eugene, as they finally left the hall.

"Yes," said Bertie. "Thank goodness it's all over."

"Until next time," said Miss Boot.

Bertie stared at her. "N-next time?"

"Of course," said Miss Boot. "That was just the first round. There's six more before you reach the final!" She thumped him hard on the back. "And we are all counting on you, Bertie!"

Out now:

DAVID ROBERTS WRITTEN BY ALAN MACDONALD

Dirty Bertie

MONSTER!

Out now:

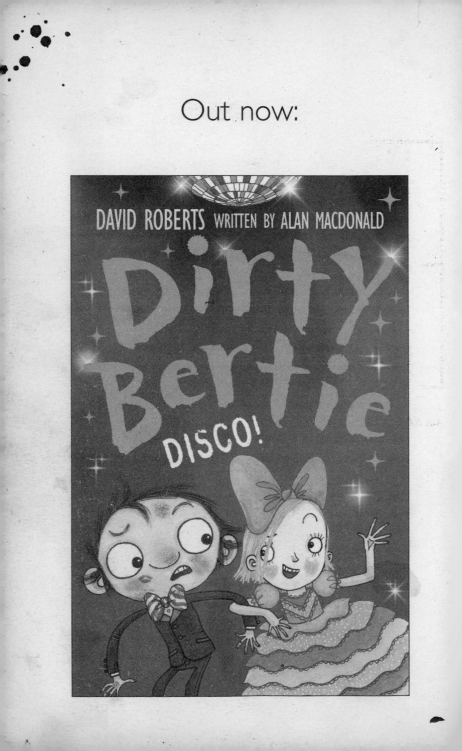